I0778951

DOCKSIDE DUCHESS

The Castleburys
Book 3

By Jennifer Seasons

© Copyright 2024 by Jennifer Seasons
Text by Jennifer Seasons
Cover by Dar Albert

Dragonblade Publishing, Inc. is an imprint of Kathryn Le Veque Novels, Inc.
P.O. Box 23
Moreno Valley, CA 92556
ceo@dragonbladepublishing.com

Produced in the United States of America

First Edition May 2024
Trade Paperback Edition

Reproduction of any kind except where it pertains to short quotes in relation to advertising or promotion is strictly prohibited.

All Rights Reserved.

The characters and events portrayed in this book are fictitious. Any similarity to real persons, living or dead, is purely coincidental and not intended by the author.

ARE YOU SIGNED UP FOR DRAGONBLADE'S BLOG?

You'll get the latest news and information on exclusive giveaways, exclusive excerpts, coming releases, sales, free books, cover reveals and more.

Check out our complete list of authors, too!

No spam, no junk. That's a promise!

Sign Up Here

www.dragonbladepublishing.com

Dearest Reader;

Thank you for your support of a small press. At Dragonblade Publishing, we strive to bring you the highest quality Historical Romance from some of the best authors in the business. Without your support, there is no 'us', so we sincerely hope you adore these stories and find some new favorite authors along the way.

Happy Reading!

CEO, Dragonblade Publishing

Additional Dragonblade books by Author Jennifer Seasons

The Castleburys Series
Mayfair Misfit (Book 1)
Duke Undone (Book 2)
Dockside Duchess (Book 3)

CHAPTER ONE

August 1832
Mayfair, London

PREPARING TO BECOME an earl and truly becoming one were two separate beasts. One felt manageable and a bit grueling, but acceptable. The other, the latter, came so suddenly, so unexpectedly, that Crawford Castlebury could only sit in his recently deceased father's study chair and look about, utterly overwhelmed. One moment the late Earl of Castlebury had been ordering his staff about, blustering and gruff—and the next he'd been clutching his chest and dropping to the ground with a startled, agonized expression on his face. Right there in the foyer of Tipton House. Heart failure, the physician had said.

Having been groomed his entire life for inheriting the title, Crawford still felt like a child wearing his father's Hessian boots. Awkward and ill-fitting.

"Come in," he called in response to the quiet knock at the door. With a broad palm, he scrubbed his hand over his face and straightened in his seat, trying to appear presentable. It was difficult to do with a crumpled, half-tied cravat hanging limp around his neck, and his hair in wild disarray from too many anxious finger-combs through it. Quickly he patted the thick auburn strands down into some semblance of order. "Door is open."

With nary a creak of the hinges, the study door silently crept open. His mother poked her head into the room, her countenance lined with grief. "I've come to inquire if you need anything. You barely touched your supper."

"Thank you, Mother." Crawford glanced at the clock on the wall and noted the time. "It's late. I'll be fine. You should get yourself some rest. I'll rummage in the kitchen if I find I'm too famished to wait until the morrow."

"Cook will make you something."

"I'll not wake him up at this hour. A rumbling stomach is a minor inconvenience that I can manage through." Noting the redness and puffiness around the countess's eyes, he realized she'd recently been crying, and softened his tone to add, "I'll be just fine, Mother. Thank you for checking on me."

"It's what mothers do." Stepping further into the room, his mother padded lightly across the plush Persian rug in bare feet. "One of several things, actually." Faded with age, her braid twisted in shades of red and gray down to her waist and swung gently with the movement. "We look after our children in myriad ways."

Something in the way his mother said the words had the hairs on the back of Crawford's neck rising in suspicion. "I would agree that is true," he cautiously offered, tilting his head to the side as he studied his mother and wondered what she was getting at.

Instead of explaining further, she went to the green velvet chaise by the fireplace and curled into it, her feet tucked neatly under her dressing gown, colored black for mourning. "I miss him." Her words were soft and honest.

"I know you do." As difficult as his father had been, his parents had truly loved each other. His children he had held less affection for.

"He was proud to be a Castlebury. Proud to be part of a family with roots deep in English soil, for generations upon generations. He did his part to carry the name and legacy forward."

A sneaking alarm crept up Crawford's spine and tingled at the back of his head. "I am aware of that…"

"You are the Earl of Castlebury now," she casually noted.

"I am." Crawford leaned back in his father's leather chair—*his* leather chair now. He narrowed his pale blue eyes slightly on his mother. "I have been the head of this family for weeks."

"And how are you faring with the transition?" His mother propped her head on her hand as she leaned against the chaise armrest, her tired blue eyes filled with genuine interest. "I have found that oft times it matters little how much preparation there has been. It is still a shock."

Crawford looked at the desk, its rich wood surface polished to a glossy sheen—and the stacks of ledgers and papers piled high and rigidly neat. Like his father. "I'm… managing?" he ventured, though he had meant it to sound a statement rather than a question.

"That is unconvincing." His mother stifled a yawn and lazily waved a hand. "How do you truly fare?"

"Well…" Crawford slid his gaze back to the stacks of estate business with equal amounts trepidation and weariness. "Father left a complicated estate to manage." He tapped a stack of leather-bound books with a finger. "The shipping business most of all."

Castle Shipping provided the estate with massive income—and several outstanding revolving debts. It was taking Crawford time to untangle the threads of his father's life—to uncover why a business generating such monumental profit should hold recurring losses of this magnitude, and to make sense of his father's business logic and rationale.

"I've spent my life up until now learning the ways of estate management and the social obligations of an elevated status, yet Father kept from me the actual mechanics of his work. These past few weeks are the first that I've gone through his ledgers. Not to speak ill of him at all, but it would have been exceedingly helpful to see actual numbers before now, to have done more than visit his office at the docklands and be given tours of the latest galleon purchased to transport spices from Bengal."

"I'm sure he had his reasons for withholding that information, dear. Perhaps he felt that such serious matters were too much for the developing mind to bear. I know not. I *do* know, however, that if anyone can figure it out, it is you. A more brilliant man I've never known—your father included, bless him." His mother briefly closed her eyes and placed a hand over her heart. Looking at Crawford once again, she continued, "You simply need a break from all the paperwork. Some fresh air, perhaps. The back gardens are particularly fragrant this time of year with all the night-blooming flowers. I had them planted specifically to help calm your father's nighttime restlessness in the hopes the aroma would soothe his nerves and let him sleep."

"Did they help?" Crawford asked quietly. On more than one occasion he had witnessed his father slipping outside after the house was quiet to pace the gardens.

A fleeting smile crossed her lips, wistful and sad. "I believe they did, to the extent anything could settle him…" His mother seemed to remember herself and started slightly, sitting up taller. "At any rate, I wanted to mention one small item before I retire to my bedchamber for the evening."

Here it comes.

Crawford mentally braced himself for the inevitable discussion, knowing full well that there would be no discussing anything. His mother would speak, and he would listen. Remain silent. He knew her lecture style well by now. He also knew the quickest, least painful way through it was to keep his mouth shut. "Yes?"

Lady Castlebury took a sudden interest in the cuticles of her nails. "It is a mother's duty to see her children settled in life. To ensure the familial line continues in smooth succession without hitch or hiccup. I'm certain you understand my meaning." She gave him a look.

"I do," Crawford murmured, sweat beading between his shoulder blades. The last thing he wanted at this point in his life was the complication of marriage. "There is plenty of time for me still, Mother. I am but eight and twenty. You needn't fear that you have failed in your maternal duty." Steepling his fingers together in front of him on the desktop, Crawford offered her his most disarming smile. "I promise you that I will fulfill that particular duty when the time is right."

Blue eyes leveled on him, startlingly sober and direct as his mother stated, "That time is now."

Pressure clamped his chest, and Crawford coughed, his lungs refusing to take in air. "I—" he croaked, his eyes watering slightly as he coughed again, struggling to breathe. "I mus—I must disagree." He coughed more and thumped his chest with a fist. "Damn," he cursed, the sound harsh as brine.

"Do not swear in front of me. It's crass."

"Apologies," Crawford wheezed, thinking a dozen more curses as he wrestled his body under control.

"Accepted." His mother yawned openly this time, her exhaustion catching up with her. "Excuse me," she murmured, and sat up, dropping her feet to the rug. "I'm more depleted than I realized."

"All is well," Crawford replied. "I understand."

"Yes, well, to return to the topic at hand, I've compiled a list of eligible young ladies of appropriate status and moral character that I should like you to utilize once your wife hunt has begun. Anyone on that list is entirely acceptable."

"Mother," he said in a low tone, "I have no intention of beginning a wife hunt."

"Then I am sorry to say that your *intention* must change. You will see this family's future secured through an appropriate marriage, an eligible heir, and a spare or two. It is your duty. As it was your father's duty before you, and his father's before him. With great fortune and breeding such as ours comes obligation and tradition and responsibility. You are no different than any other Earl of Castlebury that has gone before you. Perhaps taller, perhaps more handsome—but carrying the same burden. And like them, you will do what you must as the head of this ancient, most respectable family."

How did one argue with that?

Crawford pressed his lips into a thin, taut line, and swallowed any retort he might have had, nearly choking on it. Tonight, he was a good, *good* son. "A list, you say?" Christ, he sounded weary even to his own ears. How long had this conversation continued? An hour? A decade?

"A list!" The countess perked up considerably. "Yes, indeed. Quite the most thorough compilation of eligible young ladies that I've ever laid my eyes upon, I must confess. I truly outdid myself." She offered him a smile. "I only want the best for you, dearest."

Crawford knew that to be true. Without doubt, his mother believed that she only wished his best interest in all things. That was why it was so difficult to tell her to stop. Stop pushing, stop interfering—just stop smothering and let him breathe. "I tell you this compromise: I shall consider your list when *I* decide it is time to search for a wife."

"Hmph." The countess plucked at the hem of her sleeve and pursed her lips, appearing to contemplate something significant. "I wonder how long you think that might be?"

Never.

Oh, deuce it. Not *never*. Simply not anytime in the foreseeable future. Mayhap when he was nearing forty and had lived his life and felt a need for steadfast companionship beyond his dogs and horses. Perhaps then would be the time to search for a wife.

"In due time," he demurred, glancing out the window to the green beyond in an attempt to avoid his mother's disappointed gaze. He knew his resistance caused her strife, and it niggled at his conscience, shot darts of guilt through the pit of his belly. For she was right—it was his duty, and he should probably simply get on with it. But he could not. It was as if his heart was rooted to the ground directly along with his feet. Neither was budging anytime soon.

"Mother, are you in here?"

Crawford's attention swung to the study door in time to see his youngest sister unceremoniously shove it wide, her tall, solid figure stepping through the doorway. "She is," he quickly answered to stall Lottie, scratching his nose. The very nose broken twice his last year at Eton from an overabundance of enthusiasm and stupidity—though he did still hold the record for the highest successful tightrope walk between buildings.

That the ropes snapped before he'd completely climbed safely to the other side, and subsequently dropped three stories with the frayed ends in his hands until he smashed face-first into the red bricks of the neighboring dormitory, only added excitement and drama to the tale of how he came to possess a slightly crooked but otherwise quite aristocratic nose. The ladies said it gave him a roguish air.

How he had survived adolescence boggled him still.

"Mother, I require your opinion on this latest scene of my play, and it cannot wait until daybreak. I must know your thoughts on it this very moment!" Lottie impatiently brushed her thick, wheat-colored plait behind her shoulder with a mighty huff and thrust several worn sheets of parchment out toward the countess. "I confess I was particularly inspired by our recent viewing of Thatcher Goodrich's latest play. Brilliant though it was, I found several faults within it, and felt compelled to render the plot correctly, as it should have been. Do you know that I find Goodrich often struggles his most plot-wise in the third act? It's as if he cannot bear to bring the story to a close and therefore the crescendo loses its urgency and impact. Tsk, I say. It could be better, and so I made it thus. Oh, and pay no mind to the ink blotches and lined-through words. My mind was racing rather faster than my quill could keep up with."

"You are a peculiar child." Their mother sighed as she took possession of the small bundle and immediately began to read the first page. "A head full of stories acted out upon a stage." She shook her head. "There is no place for a lady of breeding in the theatre."

"How do you explain Carenza, then?" challenged Lottie with an arch expression, her normally quiet and steady blue eyes sparking with heat. "She is a viscountess, and she sings in Rainville's theatre quite often."

"Yes, but as the Masked Meadowlark. She has never revealed herself."

"Would it be so terrible if she did?"

"It would be a disaster!"

"Why, because then Society would know that *she* is the talent behind the extraordinary voice? The one they dote on, and lavish fanfare upon, and adore so very much? What is so very wrong with London knowing *she* is their beloved?"

"Because it is not done!" The countess jutted a finger angrily at her daughter and began to rise from the chaise. "Now, you listen quite avidly, Carlotta Castlebury. We've been over this so many times already—"

"I believe I shall take that walk you recommended, Mother," Crawford cut in, his voice forcefully loud as he pushed his chair back from the desk and rose, stretching his cramped legs. His thighs protested the movement, the strong, bulky muscles having sat idle and unused for too long. "If you'll excuse me, I shall leave you ladies to quarrel without my captive audience." Before either could cease huffing indignantly long enough to respond, he scooped up his favorite, well-worn hat from the floor, where he'd dropped it earlier and forgotten to retrieve it, plopped it on his head, and strode directly out the study doors.

"Wh-where shall you go?" His mother's belated question echoed down the hall after him.

"Wherever I shall choose," he called back as he found his jacket in the foyer and slid it over his wide shoulders and settled it into place. "As you so kindly reminded me, Mother, I *am* the earl."

"But the Revivalists!" she called out, clearly startled.

"I will be diligent and cautious, I promise." And he would be cautious. But not afraid. Time at the docklands had taught him one thing of great modern-day usefulness: how to fight. A Burmese lighterman working his father's Wapping dockland frigates had taken pity on him after seeing Crawford with one too many bloodied lips from the local chaps giving him hell. Chai had taught him that strength of body came not from muscle, but from the mind. He had taught Crawford an ancient form of Burmese self-defense known as Bando, and how to still the mind to clearly see the intentions of others. To anticipate them. These days, Crawford could handle himself.

Lottie leaned her head and upper body from the study into the hall, calling to him, "If you see Rainville, remind him he's an agreement with me to critique this play once I've completed it! Tell him that I am nearly there."

Crawford bit back a sigh. "You could tell him yourself at family dinner later this week."

"Yes, but then I would have to wait that much longer for him to know my status."

"I shall not be seeing Rainville tonight." Lottie's messenger he was not.

"Bu—"

"*However,*" he interrupted, brotherly obligation niggling him as he searched for the key he needed. Finding it in the small inside breast pocket of his olive-colored jacket, he nodded in satisfaction. "If, on the off chance that I do see him, I shall relay the message."

"Thank you," his sister primly replied with a smile, and her head disappeared back into the study.

Females.

Shaking his head, Crawford let himself out the front doors of Tipton House and began his walk. On such a rare, clear summer night as this, stars twinkled in the darkened sky. Though buffered by the light created by all of London, it still managed to lift his spirits. He breathed deeper, steadier, *easier* with each step he took that led him further and further away from familial obligation and the weight of his own grief, compounded by the heaviness of others who laid their own grief at his feet. One more burden to bear, one more to carry.

"I'm not a bloody stone," he muttered, casting an eye toward a couple strolling about a small green square fenced by low-lying shrubs blooming abundantly in shades of pink. "I *feel* things."

Why hadn't his father informed him that being the head of the family would mean so much more than merely controlling the finances?

"Could have prepared me a sight better than this, ol' chum, eh?" Crawford mused aloud, making his way through London. As if Winslow Castlebury could hear him. As if he was standing right there next to him, with his disapproving glower and glacial judgment, instead of lying prone and stiff six feet underground in Westminster Abbey. "What have you gotten me into?"

The sudden stench brought him out of his musings, the Thames close by now as he rounded a corner on a narrow street in Wapping and headed toward the infamous Prospect of Whitby. A tall pint and some lively entertainment could be just the thing he needed. If perhaps there was more than a small element of risk in attending the Prospect, then perhaps one could extrapolate that Crawford willingly assumed said risk. Mayhap even embraced it.

Sometimes even an earl needed to enjoy some rough entertainment and release tension from all those burdens weighing him down.

"Heya, watch it, mister!"

Crawford jerked away, his arm buzzing from the impact of ramming into the stranger currently glaring and cursing at him. "Apologies," he mumbled, casting the small man a distracted glance. "Beg your pardon." Dockworker, he noted, knowing instantly the man's occupation. It was the clothes, yes. But also the way the small man moved, agile and fleet-footed. So much time spent at the London Docks during his youth had taught Crawford to recognize such things.

"Yeah, yeah," the dockworker grumbled, glaring up at him with startlingly green eyes, big as teacup saucers and just as round under a set of dark, arching brows. Crawford jolted at the intensity found there and coughed, feeling oddly self-conscious. "Out of the way, toff."

Toff?

Crawford was no toff! Oh, but wait. He *was*. "As you wish," he replied, dipping his chin low, acknowledging the worker's request—without drama or fanfare or fuss. Because sometimes life required confrontation. But most often, it did not if one didn't let it. And he did not wish to let it. Chai had taught him well the importance of separating oneself from one's ego and pride. Besides, the man barely reached his shoulder. It wouldn't be fair.

With a huff and another glare of those startling green eyes, the short dockworker passed, muttering words that Crawford couldn't understand. He watched as the man went, his gaze fixed on the worker's stride, noting with curiosity a rather delicate sway of hip.

"Huh," Crawford said, and turned his attention to the old pub coming into view up ahead. A drink or three were in order.

Whatever it took to shake the looming shackles of earldom and his mother's "list" from his mind.

CHAPTER TWO

S LAPPING TWO COINS on the scarred bar top, Sadie Crisp paid her tab and drank down the last drops of ale from her pint glass. When coin was sparse, it paid to wring every last drop of drink through to the very last sip. "Appreciate it," she muttered in a low, affected voice, wiping the back of a stained sleeve across her mouth. Mindful to keep her words short and concise, she added to the barkeep with a tip of her brown cap, "Cheers."

"Ungh," the barkeep grunted back with a quick glance of acknowledgment.

"Leaving so soon, Baker?" called a dockworker from a booth along the back wall of the Prospect of Whitby, one of London's oldest and most notorious pubs. History went that loads of hangings had happened right off the old docks, with the pub's patrons settled on the balconies, enjoying the show. Stories passed down claimed they'd toasted and drunk to every pirate and lawbreaker when that noose stretched taut on Execution Dock.

A rougher crowd could hardly be found.

And Sadie Crisp, duchess in hiding, felt exactly at home.

"Go piss up a tree," she suggested in response to the drunken lighterman she knew well from working the Commercial Docks in Rotherhithe across the Thames from Wapping and the Prospect. "I'd load your sculler full of crates faster than you, and you well know it. Not my fault that all that ale you consume makes you slow and sloppy."

"Now, you see here, Thomas Baker," the lighterman hic-cupped, too far into his cups to do anything more than holler and act belligerent.

Briefly, Sadie fought the urge to sit down and play a few rounds of cards against the drunk just to fleece him for the satisfaction of it. But then she thought of the walk home and the current time. With a sigh, she regretfully passed on the cards and waved to the dockworker in the back booth. "See you at Canada Docks on the morrow, Dom. Big timber shipment from the Baltic coming in."

"Best eat your meat, then, kid. You're still too scrawny for deal porter work."

Sadie took offense at that. "Who carried more loads of fresh and heavy raw-cut deal today? Me or you, eh?" Her voice began to rise in pitch, and she coughed, shoving her fists into the front pockets of her trousers. With her shoulders hunching defensively, she glared at Dom.

The gruff, raven-haired dockworker waved his beefy hands, chuckling. It sounded rather like glass grinding underfoot. "You win, Baker."

"Maybe you should eat more vegetables," Sadie shot out, and flashed Dom a tight smile. "Then you could keep up with me."

"Suck my tree trunk, Baker."

Sadie chuckled despite herself and shoved the front door of the Prospect open wide, grateful for the evening breeze outside that greeted her. She held up her pinky finger and waggled it over her shoulder. "Don't be telling lies, Dom. We all know it's more like a twig than a trunk."

Laughter erupted inside the Prospect of Whitby, and Sadie smirked. Served Dom right for harassing her.

As she stepped into the August night, the door shut with a click behind her. To her right was the ol' hanging dock, looking rather ominous as fog rolled in off the Thames and crawled in thin fingers across the cobblestoned street in front of her. Above her, swinging right along with the Prospect's sign, was a noose to commemorate all those strung necks. Because that made sense. Nothing said "welcome and have a drink" like a death warning.

Englishmen.

Bloodthirsty lot.

Sadie frowned, her thoughts turning to one bloodthirsty Englishman in particular. A shiver snaked down her spine, and she flipped up the collar of her worn tweed workman's jacket, hunkered deep into it. How she hated being afraid of him. Cousin Archibald. Wasn't family supposed to mean something? Be safe? Between him and the Revivalists, London's streets were always a gamble, always a risk. No telling when either might strike. And after close encounters she'd had with both, she was in no rush to ever experience them again. Ever. Again.

Somewhere in the far distance a horn blew, the sound undoubtedly belonging to a ship past port struggling to navigate in the thick fog. Still, the sound echoed with a melancholic note that reverberated inside Sadie's chest and had tears springing to her eyes.

"Damn it," she cursed, and blinked them back. Getting caught crying like a girl when she was supposed to be a man would cause far more trouble than it was worth. "Dry it up," Sadie ordered herself. Wimps got dead. That was the saying down at the docks. Good and helpful if she remembered that.

Wimps got dead.

Casting a glance up and down the cobbled street in front of her, Sadie crossed when all appeared empty, the fog lapping greedily at her booted ankles as she made her way inland and away from the docks toward her tiny flat in Cheapside. Little more than an attic room with a fireplace and small kitchen set above a haberdashery, it was nevertheless home. More importantly, it was safe. Hidden. Where no one would search for the newly titled Duchess of Seawell: Her Grace Sadie Windcrisp, otherwise known as Miss Sadie Crisp—or so she signed on the signature lines. To her coworkers at Rotherhithe's Docks, she was simply Thomas Baker, the young—male—lightweight deal porter from Whitechapel.

Layers of identity, layers of protection from a relative—from *family*—who desired her dead, simply to claim her fortune and title for himself.

"Bastard sickened me with my own tea." Once Sadie had realized what her cousin was about, she had enlisted the help of her maid in procuring the herbs necessary to heal from the toxin she had ingested. Afterward, she had disappeared. Sick and weak and still feverish, she'd stolen away in the black of night with the small sack of herbs, a secret stash of money, and those precious papers detailing her claim to the duchy, written by her beloved father, the Duke of Seawell, before his death.

"Oomph." Something solid and large rammed into Sadie's shoulder, shocking her from her mental ramblings. "Heya, watch it, mister!" she snapped.

"Apologies," a deep, cultured male voice murmured. "Beg your pardon."

Alarmed at her lack of attentiveness to her surroundings, Sadie looked up to the stranger's countenance, shadowed by the low lamplight dotting the narrow street. A gasp formed in her throat, and she hastily swallowed it, her eyes locked on the most arresting face she had ever seen. Slashing, commanding eyebrows were set over thick-lashed eyes of such crystalline clarity that they glowed like blue flames in the flickering lantern light. They stared down at her, directly into her soul. Pierced her there.

Reeling from the sensation, Sadie glared and jerked a shoulder. "Out of the way, toff," she grumbled, pushing past the man who was obviously an aristocrat. She would recognize High Society breeding anywhere, but especially in a face such as that one. Sharp cheekbones and an arrogant chin, stubborn mouth. Toff features, through and through.

She should know. She bore them herself.

Tugging her flat workman's cap further down on her head, mindful to keep her long brown strands tucked securely underneath, Sadie set off once more to her tiny bit of home comfort in Cheapside.

"Hmm, interesting," she heard the toff comment, his blue-fire gaze boring into her back. The intensity of his scrutiny sent her feet shuffling and her pace quickening. *Nothing of interest to see, nothing at all of interest,* Sadie reiterated in her mind as she scuttled away from the man's penetrating pale eyes, the skin between her shoulder blades hot and itching. After several steps, she glanced back over her shoulder, something compelling her to seek the aristocrat out one more time. Thankfully, his attention had turned from her to the Prospect at the end of the lane on the riverfront.

Without thought, she swept her gaze over the nobleman's body, from his shining brown riding boots to his hat—a slightly frayed and crumpled, short hat, the color of which had once been a light gray. Now it appeared to have collected a fair bit of coal dust around its seams, shading portions of its brim a deep charcoal.

Life in London was rarely clean.

Much the same could be said of its people.

Scowling at that thought, Sadie let her gaze wander up the toff's legs until she discovered herself greedily soaking in the sight of his thick, muscular thighs encased in a pair of snug riding breeches.

"Stop that," she muttered to herself. "They're simply legs. They serve a purpose. Thick thighs deserve no more adulation than thin ones."

Not true, a voice in her mind whispered. *They deserve the* most *appreciation.*

With a silent groan and not a little reluctance, Sadie pulled her attention from the toff's surprisingly attractive backside and his directed, confident walk. Losing her wits at the sight of an inspiring pair of thighs while the Revivalists were still on the loose was undoubtedly a foolish risk to take. She knew personally how quickly they attacked, lucky to have merely been knocked unconscious the night they took the Masked Meadowlark. The murderers could swoop upon her before she had cleared the thick-thigh infatuation from her eyes. And that would not do. Not do at all.

Of all people, Sadie knew better than to let her guard down. The last time had nearly killed her. "I'll not meet my demise because of clouded vision."

With that promise on her lips, she slipped quietly and quickly the rest of the way home to Cheapside. Though "home" was a relative term, she supposed. Her actual address was deep in the heart of Mayfair, near Hyde Park. Not far, in truth, from the duke recently married to her closest friend, Lady Carenza's younger sister Nora—the nobleman His Grace Joss Rainville, Duke of Somerton. Their London townhomes resided only a narrow street or two away from one another. Yet he did not know that fact. Nor did he know that she, Sadie Crisp, was in any way related to the Windcrisps of Park Lane.

Which was exactly how she'd planned it.

And exactly as it would remain.

No one to know, no one the wiser—no one coming for her. Sadie remained alive. Inheritance or not, *alive* qualified as her most vital necessity. Money she could earn, and a roof over her head she could provide for herself. But only if she remained breathing.

With that uplifting thought accompanying her, she hurried on and reached her destination, sighing a hefty gust of relief when she spotted it. "Home." Sadie looked up at the three-story brick haberdashery building and could have wept at the comforting sight. Her five-floor Mayfair townhouse it was not. But Cousin Archibald did not reside within these walls, and that made the haberdasher shop and its tiny flat atop it the most perfect, lovely accommodation upon the earth.

Sadie had taken two steps up the flight of stairs past the owner of the shop's own flat, located directly above the haberdashery, when the gray-haired German woman stuck her head into the hall and blinked large, owl-like eyes behind her round spectacles. "Herr Baker," Frau Olsen greeted Sadie in her efficient voice. "I have worried for you and your *Frau*, out so late with those, those *Kriminelles* terrorizing the good people of this city." The round-shouldered, ample woman cast her gaze up and down the hall. "Where is your *Schnucki*, hmm?"

Sadie bit back a tart reply, tired after a day of hauling deal, her right shoulder giving her fits from the hefty loads upon it. All she wished was some quiet and her bed. Not a well-meaning-but-intrusive widow with little else to do to occupy her mind but fuss over her "neighbors." It had taken no time at all to realize that correcting Frau Olsen's notion that she, Sadie, was somehow a married couple (and not a single person coming and going as two separate people) would be far more hassle than it was worth.

Sadie thought quickly and pitched her voice low to say, "She is unwell and stayed abed resting today." She believed that fabrication would do. If she recalled correctly, she had only appeared in public today as Baker for her shift at Rotherhithe. Or had she enjoyed morning tea on her tiny balcony in her dressing gown? Days passed by in such a busy, blurry haze that she scarcely remembered anymore.

"Goodness! That will not do. She shall have turnip stew to aid her recovery. I will add much garlic." Frau Olsen nodded decisively and disappeared, slamming the door closed. Through the solid plank, Sadie could hear the German woman muttering to herself as pots began to clang about.

Sadie found her hand fisted and raised, ready to bang upon the door, when she realized that any attempt to stop the elderly woman would be futile. Since the passing of her husband, there had not been many people in Frau Olsen's life over which she could fuss and care. The turnip soup was as much for her as it was for Sadie.

Her stomach growled, gnawing and suddenly ravenous at the thought of food. *When was the last time I ate?* Sadie wondered as she continued up the stairs to her tiny flat. Ale at the Prospect of

Whitby didn't count.

Then perhaps the last time she had eaten was…

It had to have been…

Well, she *had* eaten breakfast… hadn't she?

Sadie reached her door and stopped, grimacing at her lack of proper care for herself.

Perhaps the soup would be good for her, too. Bless Frau Olsen's lonely, fussy old heart. "Sometimes being alone is rotten," Sadie muttered in a moment of shared understanding with the widow downstairs.

Slipping into her miniscule haven at the top of a store filled with baubles and buttons and pins—and everything possible in between—she felt the weight, the constant pressure, shift and ease. Tears immediately sprang to Sadie's eyes, tears that came from such weary gratitude for the simple blessing of *ease*. Finally, for one more day, she was at ease.

Wiping at a tear streaking hot and heavy down her cheek, Sadie slumped against her front door, safely cocooned within her wee flat. She felt the sadness that she kept buried, the old one she had tamped way deep down inside, stir. "A bloody duchess hiding in a dockworker's clothes." Ripping off her cap, she threw it on the seat of the only cushioned chair in the room, feeling the heavy, glossy strands of her hair cascade in waves to her waist. "Who would have thought my life would turn out like this?" Her waistcoat came next, joining her cap on the tatty upholstered chair. "I don't need fine silks or fancy silver with which to dine on sweetmeats. But I do want to live without fear for my life every bloody moment that I breathe."

The constant vigilance was exhausting.

If only Sadie had been born a male. None of this would be happening if she were a man. Her parents would have died, and the title and inheritance would have descended accordingly. She would have assumed the title of duke, and the entailed fortune and estates would squarely be hers.

"But if you possess breasts and a womb, you own nothing,

not even your own birthright." The words sounded as bitter on her tongue as they tasted.

"*Frau!* Oh, Frau Baker! I have stew for you."

Sadie's stomach clamped hard in hunger. "Thank you!" she called out in her own voice, thankful for something hot and nourishing to eat. "I'll be there directly!" Swiping her face dry with the palms of her hands, she shook her hair loose about her shoulders, stepped away from the door, and turned to it to crack it open.

"Oh, *Frau*, I had been informed you were unwell, but your Herr Baker did not tell me how truly awful you look!" The elderly woman held up a covered container, frowning as she assessed Sadie's appearance. "This will help."

"It's much appreciated, Frau Olsen, thank you." Sadie snaked a hand around the door and grasped the still-warm container, trying not to take offense. Undoubtedly, she did appear a haggard sight. It had been a long day. "I'll be certain to return the jar."

"Such a dear you are—"

"Have a good evening!" Sadie interjected, and began to close the door. "Thank you again for the soup!"

"Stew, my dear. It is stew… Goodness, are you wearing Herr Baker's *clothes?*"

Sadie glanced down at her linen tunic, her eyes rounding with alarm over being caught in her deal porter clothing. "Um," she sputtered, thinking of an excuse—any excuse. "It, uh, helps comfort me when I'm feeling unwell."

"For me it was Herr Olsen's stockings," Frau Olsen said with suddenly misty eyes as the door shut with a click between them. "Good eve and good health, Frau Baker!"

"Good eve and good health!" Sadie called back, already unscrewing the container lid, the lure of hot, home-cooked food making her forget her unfortunate life circumstances in the face of one very real, very tangible fact: Sadie might not have her duchy, but somebody had cared enough about her to see her properly fed.

Dropping the lid on the tiny kitchen table, she snatched a spoon and dug in, grateful.

Tonight, that was enough.

CHAPTER THREE

"**I**T'S A BEAUTIFUL day to be quayside, milord."

"Indeed, it is," Crawford replied to his companion, squinting against the glare of the morning sun reflecting off the Thames. The water flowed particularly smooth today, turning its surface into a natural, glossy mirror. It was lovely.

If one could get beyond the stench.

"How do you manage it?" Feeling his nose begin to twitch, Crawford pressed a finger as nonchalantly as he could to the side of one nostril, willing it still.

"The stink, you mean?" the dockworker replied, hooking his thumbs into the front of his suspenders. "Ah, you get used to it." With a well-aimed spit, he added, "Hell's bells, I ain't e'en notice it no more. Near smells good."

Crawford would not gag. He would not. No, he would... *Ah, hell.*

"Pay no mind, milord—you ain't the first to 'ave tha' reaction, and you won' be the last. She's an acquired odor, our Thames. 'Specially up close like she is now."

"Yes, well," Crawford murmured, blinking eyes gone watery from the strength of the scent. "Why don't we take a tour of Castle Shipping and all that it entails? Perhaps we could start across the Thames at the Surrey Commercial Docks, where a new shipment of timber from America is scheduled to be unloaded."

"Ah, tha'll smell a might finer, fer certain." The dockworker chuckled. "Fresh-cut pine will clear the nostrils of all the stink. Come along."

"I've spent much of my life down here at the docklands," Crawford started, eagerly following the worker. "Well, mostly in Wapping at the company's warehouse on the North Quay in my father's office, or on a galleon learning to tie knots—but here in this location. I do not recall the river's scent being so offensive. Is it me, or has the unpleasant odor intensified these past few years?"

"Oh no, milord, it's no' just you. Loads of London's poor been using the Thames as a loo, and tha's gone an' mucked wi' wots growin' in it. Now we got shite water and God knows wot else floating about."

Crawford's step faltered, and he cast a dubious glance at the murky water lapping quietly mere feet from his Hessians, just a few short inches lower than the wooden dock currently keeping him separate and dry. It wasn't that he minded being wet. He minded becoming wet by water filled with more shite than fish.

"Tell me," Crawford said as he stepped behind two men hauling heavy-looking barrels and swearing mightily, doing his best to keep pace with the fleet-footed dockworker touring him about his holdings. "How long have you been working at Castle Shipping?"

The young man glanced over his shoulder, seeming to consider. "Since Christmastide last, I suppose. Directly after the festivities."

"Did you know my father well?" Crawford sidestepped a man loaded down with wooden crates. Quick reflexes kept them both out of the Thames.

Crawford smiled to himself. Moments such as these were when Chai deserved a rather large expression of gratitude for teaching him stealth and balance as a lad. All those sharp corrections from the Burmese monk-turned-lighterman had taught him well and come in useful upon more occasions than he could possibly count.

Moving swiftly over the giant, flat gray stones lining the quays, the dockworker disappeared for a moment between stacks of crates that were on their way to the enormous brick warehouse directly to Crawford's left. "This way, milord!" he called, poking a hand above the wooden boxes to wave at him.

"Everything is fine," Crawford muttered to himself quietly, picking up his pace, trying without much success to ignore the looming cloud of pressure lurking just over his shoulder. "It's fine. Completely and utterly fine." He could and would manage this company well.

As soon as he figured out how.

"Thank you for showing me about on such short notice." Crawford reached the dockworker's side again, striding strongly and purposefully to keep up. "I apologize for not inquiring after your name before now. Inexcusably rude of me. And you are?"

"Name's Charlie Woodmill, milord, at your service." The dockworker stuck out a hand and gave Crawford's a sturdy shake. Not a curtsy, but a handshake. How refreshing. "Too bad wot got Dobbs killed. Ne'er heard of a shark in the Thames this far up afore. No I 'aven't."

With a grimace of sympathy for Castle Shipping's recently deceased operations manager, Crawford agreed, wiggling his fingers unconsciously over the bizarre accident. "Have there been any spotted since?" His eyes were locked on the water. Of course they were—a bloomin' *shark* had taken a bite out of Dobbs big enough to expose his spine when the poor chap had the misfortune of tumbling from the plank of a galleon unloading rice from the Qing district of China. Both Dobbs and his ever-present clipboard that tallied the receipt of goods had ended up inside the belly of the ocean's fiercest beast.

To this day, they still had no idea how much rice had truly been delivered on that shipment. Or how a vicious shark had swum that far up the river.

They had lost an efficient, perfunctory man that day. Diminutive of stature but mighty with mathematics. Who would Crawford ever find to replace Dobbs's skill with arithmetic and recordkeeping?

"Say…" he began, casting a considering glance at Woodmill as they reached the end of a wide quay and began to make their way down a much smaller side dock to a waiting vessel. It appeared miniscule compared to the mighty frigates making berth behind them. "You wouldn't happen to have a knack for bookkeeping, would you?"

Woodmill laughed with a shake of his shaggy brown head and motioned Crawford in front of him. "No' e'en a smidge, milord. I'm rubbish wi' tha' sort o' thing. Me mum and da sent me to work afore I could count past the fingers on me 'and."

Swallowing his shock at the brevity of Woodmill's youth, Crawford stepped onto the boat and took a seat, his heart beating perhaps a tiny fraction faster than his ego preferred it. But two weeks ago, a shark had miraculously swum upstream in the brackish estuary water of the Thames and eaten a man. Bits and pieces of Dobbs might still be flittering about below the surface.

"Oh God." Crawford blanched and shuddered at the gruesome thought. His stomach lurched uneasily.

Today was determined to see him cast up his breakfast.

"If this morning is indicative of the general tone of my ownership term, I will gladly pass." Enough problems plagued him of late. More of them were the last thing he needed.

"Worry no', milord. It will get better." Woodmill offered him a reassuring smile, his teeth surprisingly strong and white in his sun-weathered countenance. "Now, come along. We'll be across the Thames and slipped into Rotherhithe afore you can gather your sea legs."

"Sea legs I have." Crawford frowned, gripping the railing firmly as the vessel moved away from its mooring. "It's legs of inedible steel that I have not." He scanned the muddy surface of the Thames, searching discreetly for a dorsal fin. If it could happen to Dobbs, it could happen to him.

Crawford shifted away from the water.

While he was preoccupied with the hypothetical possibility of a second shark in the Thames waiting under the surface of the water to disembowel him, they navigated the cross traffic and had reached Canada Yard before Crawford realized they'd even set out. "Impressive," he murmured with his arms crossed. It never ceased to amaze him how deft at navigation watermen truly were.

"Ah, 'ere we are, milord! Up ahead you'll see tha' huge stack of raw timber coming down off tha' barque cargo ship." Woodmill gestured to a tall, impeccably tidy stack of lumber to his left. "Our deal porters put it 'ere afore it gets moved into the warehouse for storage and wot 'ave you."

"And what is that?" Crawford inquired, pointing to an interesting contraption jutting up and over the water.

"Tha's a crane built for lifting full logs off the ship, milord." Woodmill tilted his head back to survey the giant structure as the sculler drifted smoothly through the yard, seeking a place to moor. "Heya, Baker, mind the swing of 'er!" The dockworker winced as he shouted to a small man standing atop a pile of planks near the head of the crane. "Berta will kick your bollocks up your throat an' dump you in the Thames. An' I ain't divin' in after wot ate Dobbs!"

"Don't go blaming that shark! Too little rain and too much salt mixing in the headways of the Thames creating confusion for those beasts, Woodmill, you know that. Sends 'em upriver when they're hungry."

"Wot you, a fancy-arse naturalist?" Woodmill shot back with a grin, making his way upside a solid-looking dock, bumping the side of the sculler when he pulled in close to tie off.

"Fancier than you!" shouted down the deal porter as he side-stepped and cleared way for the crane to rotate a log as big around as Crawford's dining room table. Agile and nimble, the light-footed Baker hopped from plank to plank until well clear of the bark-stripped log. "*I can count without taking off my shoes!*"

Laughing, Woodmill hopped from the sculler onto the dock. "You should take over Dobbs's job, then!"

Alerted by those words, Crawford forgot momentarily about what might be lurking under the water's surface and glanced up with interest. He did need a replacement for Dobbs, as it were. Could this man fill the role? "Mr. Baker," he repeated quietly, remembering the name for later as he too climbed from the boat. Relief swept through him at once again being on solid footing.

Several workers glanced Crawford's way as he began to walk with Woodmill through the waterside lumber yard, most of them returning quickly to their work to avoid unwanted conversation. Nobody wanted to talk with the owner.

"Who's this shiny bloke?"

Perhaps, except, for one.

"This 'ere is the new owner of Castle Shipping." Woodmill gestured to Crawford, his attention atop the stack of lumber on Baker. "The Earl of Castlebury."

"So, you're the dandy." The deal porter seemed to assess him from his perch several feet up. "Been lots of chatter about you."

Crawford squinted against the sun to focus on the short man, briefly debating how best to respond. But then something compelled him to be blunt and needling. "Odd—there's been none at all about you." Shoving his hands in the front pocket of his breeches, he shot the deal porter a smug glance. "Seems one of our reputations precedes us."

"That isn't the compliment you think it is," Baker shot back.

"Ha!" Damnation, but Crawford did like a good verbal sparring. "If you're going to make jests of me, then you must come down here and properly introduce yourself."

"And if I don't?" Baker challenged, one dark brow quirked.

"Then I will simply have to come up." Glancing at the vertical stacks of lumber, Crawford realized there was no *simple* about it.

"You'll ruin my whole bloody system, you do that," Baker grumbled, uncrossing his arms with a gusty sigh. "Stay put—I'll come down."

And with that, Baker bent, contorted his compact body, and shimmied down that pile of lumber at a mind-boggling pace. Crawford's entire body tensed with nerves as he watched on, absurdly concerned for the wee fellow. When the dockworker dropped silently to the ground before him, agile as a cat, Crawford blurted, "How in devil's fire do you do that?"

"Any gob with decent balance can do it."

"Now that's a bouncer, if I e'er heard one!" called Woodmill over his shoulder from further down the stacks of lumber. "None but you be pullin' tha' stunt." The dockworker stood in conversation with a group of lightermen tasked with unloading grain from a five-masted ship named the *Drunken Mermaid*.

"Don't tell me…" Crawford glanced toward the bow and the figurehead there. "Of course," he murmured, seeing the bare-breasted mermaid with strategically placed red hair over her nipples, and the pint of ale in her fist. She held it aloft in front of her as if giving the ocean a celebratory toast. "My father's personal favorite vessel, no doubt."

"Actually, that would be that galleon over there." Baker appeared next to him and pointed across the yard to an enormous Spanish ship with the largest set of windows along the back of the captain's quarters that Crawford had ever seen. "He said *Susanna's Secret* was a special lady to him."

Hair at the base of Crawford's neck prickled and stirred.

Susanna was his mother's name.

Interesting.

Crawford considered the mighty galleon several moments longer before glancing down to Baker. Shock rippled through him when his gaze met the greenest eyes he had ever seen. Well, met *again*. "Of all the people," Crawford murmured, recognition dawning.

"Yes," the deal porter quietly agreed, a wry note in his tone. Standing directly next to Crawford, his head barely reached his shoulder. "Seems we meet again."

"So it seems." For a dockworker, Baker had surprisingly dewy-looking skin, Crawford couldn't help noticing. Was the lad even old enough to shave? Crawford could detect no stubble. Not even a shadow beard.

"What are you looking at?" the deal porter asked defensively.

Crawford wasn't quite sure. Something was not adding up properly for him. There appeared inconsistencies to Baker.

"Heya, don't put that there!" Baker scowled and stomped away in a huff, attention squarely on another worker carrying a barrel over his shoulder. "You know if it's snuff, it gets unloaded at the tobacco dock. We only do the timber here. Leave it aboard, Smully."

Narrowing his eyes in keen interest, Crawford watched on, noting with fascination once again that rather feminine swaying of hips as Baker strode across the dock shouting orders at the man named Smully. But Crawford was not paying attention to the words. Oh no, he was paying a lot of attention to the plump, shapely derriere protruding from the deal porter's backside.

"Wait a minute…" he murmured, the hairs on the back of his neck rising in suspicion.

Feminine sway of hip…

Shapely, plump backside…

Smooth facial skin with nary a trace of stubble…

Huge, round green eyes that set his pulse racing…

"Good God," he breathed as the realization hit him. It was the only possible explanation. More to the point, it was obvious if one took the moment to look. "Mr. Baker is a woman."

A *woman*.

Every protective instinct in Crawford sprang to life with a mighty force, and he stopped himself before shouting at her to be careful, as climbing timber stacks was no place for a female.

What stopped him? The truth. Because clearly it *was* a place for a female.

Baker was there.

Baker. Green-eyed Baker. Shapely arsed Baker.

Female Baker.

Arousal rose suddenly and slammed into Crawford with the force of a hurricane. It cut his breath, weakened his knees, held him captive as he watched this disguised woman shimmy and climb her way up a twenty-foot stack of timber to stand confidently at the top. Like she belonged there. Never in all his years at the docklands had he ever witnessed such finesse, such acrobatic strength and agility.

And it came from a woman.

Crawford's knees gave out, and he plunked down on the dock, folding his legs under him. A woman hid on his docks as a deal porter. And females were not allowed to work on the docks. There were rules. Regulations. *Laws.* What if she got hurt? What then? What if the other workers discovered her? Christ, it would be like bloody pirates discovering a lass aboard their ship. They might mutiny. Deuce it, he couldn't afford that.

What was he to do?

Crawford smashed his hat further on his head and glanced up at the woman known as Baker. He considered for several moments before deciding. *If she's here hiding, it's for a reason.*

Best plan of action was to do nothing. Simply sit back and see what unfolded. If his workers found out about her, well, he would deal with them accordingly, if, and when, the time came.

And here he'd thought it couldn't get any more dangerous than a shark in the Thames.

He should have prepared for a woman.

CHAPTER FOUR

S ADIE FINISHED HER shift at the docks and disappeared as quickly and quietly as she could, her stomach lodged in her throat. Good God, the way the new owner looked at her! Heart pounding, she decided the hell with frugality and hired a hack to take her across London Bridge to Covent Garden and a narrow, dodgy alley behind her second favorite place in this new world of hers: the Meadowlark Tavern. The pub stood as bastion between the depravity seeping deep within the garden, and the vibrant commerce and life of Covent Garden itself.

Importantly, her friends were there.

Most of them, at any rate. Carenza certainly wouldn't be there, newly married and titled and all. And her husband, Damon, would not be in attendance, either. Come to that, neither would Rainville. Probably. The golden duke with his obnoxious sense of grandiosity somehow managed to belong to a select few people she deemed her friends.

Which left her with her last chum, West. If the owner and barkeep of the tavern wasn't there tonight, then she was in trouble. *Perhaps I need more friends.* Or perhaps she could use a poke in the eye with a jagged stick, for that was how much that notion appealed to her.

"Frau Olsen is my friend," she asserted aloud. See? That made a grand total of four. Four perfectly acceptable people to call comrades. Who in blazes needed more than that? *Too much bloody work.*

Besides, Sadie was in hiding. More blokes calling themselves her friend meant more chances of discovery. And that was not happening. She would stay alive. Alive and in control of her own fortune, title, and destiny.

Oh, why can't he simply fall in a hole and die? No one would miss Cousin Archibald and his pedantic ways. Society might even be a bit relieved, truth be told, if they discovered news of his demise. His presence at any gathering brought the entirety of the room down, like the snuffing of a candle. All the light disappeared in a flash, casting everything and everyone in shadowed gloom. Even before her discovery of his murderous intentions toward her, Sadie had known something sinister lurked beneath the surface of his character. Thankfully, her father had agreed with her assessment of him and denied Archibald's offer of marriage to her last Season, on the grounds of Archibald being her first cousin. Though it was not forbidden expressly by law, her father wished no close relations for Sadie's husband, and had clarified in writing his preference for his only child.

Hence her tea laced with deadly *digitalis.*

"Are you going to stand out there all night staring at nothing like a buffoon, or are you coming inside for a drink?"

A slow grin split Sadie's face. "I missed you too, West."

"Sure you did." The burly American waved her inside. "Now hustle on in. Foolish to stand out here all alone in the dark with the Revivalists out. Been talks tonight about their latest attack."

Bugger. "They struck again?" Hadn't London dealt with enough already? Carenza's brother Catamount and his Bow Street Runners needed to capture those abominations once and for all. Though, to be fair, Bow Street's lack of success wasn't from refusing to try. They'd even caught one of the Revivalist members a while back when he took Carenza from the Meadowlark, but he'd killed himself before confessing information. Sadie had been fortunate to escape that night with only a lump on her head and a headache the size of Hampshire.

She'd *kept* her head. And that mattered. A duchess couldn't run an estate from the grave.

"They attacked last night over in St. Giles." West's alert gaze scanned the alley behind her. "Come on in and I'll tell you more about it."

Did she really want to know?

No, but she needed to. Information and knowledge kept her safe.

"You so concerned you want to send everyone home?" Sadie stepped past West into the welcoming interior of the tavern. Old, worn wood beams and scarred oak floors greeted her, along with the scents of ale and tobacco smoke and wood fire. "If so, is it too late to get something from the kitchen to fill my belly before I head out?"

"For you, no. Everyone else, maybe, yeah. Let me think if it's worth trying to close the Meadowlark without proof of imminent threat. Not sure it's worth the ruckus it'll cause. All you English are a stubborn lot, you know that?"

Sadie laughed, thankful for the privacy of the tavern's back rooms and the long central hall they strode down, knowing West kept secrets better than anybody. Not once had he asked her to explain why she often appeared at the pub dressed in men's work clothes. He'd only ever asked her to let him help when the time came. Like he understood her.

West was uncanny that way.

"We English prefer to live life fully and for the moment." Tomorrow came as no guarantee. Drink, live, love *today*. Ask any red-blooded Englishman, and he would tell you that.

"The operative word is 'live' there, Sadie," the tavern owner drawled, his brawny shoulders comfortingly large and capable behind her. "Don't know about you, but getting stabbed by one of them bastards the night they took Carenza was more than enough excitement for me. I'm in no rush to feel that burning-fire gut spillage ever again."

Sadie winced at his crude description and glanced back at

him. "Damnation, West. You have to describe it in detail like that?"

The bartender shrugged, his gray eyes serious. "That's what it felt like."

"I'm glad you made it." The words came out of Sadie in a rush of honesty.

"Me too." Gratitude flowed through his two words.

"Before we step through the door here," Sadie started, her hand on the doorknob, "is there anyone I should be on alert about?" She tipped her head toward the heavy wooden door that separated the public portion of the tavern from the private one. "I've been having a strange, antsy feeling all day. Makes me itchy, you know?"

It had nothing at all to do with a pair of ice-fire blue eyes rimmed with thick, lush lashes sooty as coal. The last thing she could possibly care about was the new owner of Castle Shipping. *Toff. Pretty-eyed dandy.*

But was he, though?

Toff, yes. Pretty-eyed, yes. Dandy?

Well... He *was* dressed rather nicely in masculine, subtle hues befitting the description. Yet the new earl didn't seem particularly witty or charming, and that was an important requirement for the makings of a proper dandy.

"I don't think there's much to concern yourself with tonight, other than the regulars churned up a little extra over the Revivalists' attack."

Sadie steeled herself with a deep, fortifying breath and turned the doorknob, glancing over her shoulder at West. "Tell me."

He knew exactly what she was talking about. "Three killed and a doxy left in such unrecognizable condition that no one can identify her. She ain't expected to make it to dawn."

"Damn it!" Sadie said, her stomach twisting sourly. "God-damn it, West."

"I know it," he quietly replied, the heaviness of his spirit over the violence weighing down his every word.

"They have to be stopped." Someone needed to do it. *Anybody*.

"Hard to stop apparitions when you can't see them coming."

Though she didn't like it, West's words held truth. The murderous group of aristocrats slipped out of the London fog like monsters from a nightmare, attacking everything and anything in their reach. Business buildings set on fire, houses wrecked, properties destroyed, women harmed in body and spirit and left broken for dead. Men and women killed for sport, chased to ground like foxes.

"Point made," Sadie mumbled, a sliver of apprehension shivering down her spine. "Figure out who one of them is and we can figure out the rest."

"Now, that ain't exactly true, Sadie, you know that. They caught Amslee, but we still don't know who the others are."

"That's only because the bastard killed himself before anyone could make him confess." And he wasn't missed.

"You doing all right?" West asked from behind her. "You seem extra prickly tonight."

"Yeah, I guess I am." Sadie blew out her breath and shook her shoulders loose, then rolled her head to ease the tension in her neck. "It's been a day."

West reached a big, beefy arm over her head and grasped the door, swinging it open. "Then go on in and grab a pint." Noise and jovial activity greeted them on the other side.

"And a pasty?" she asked hopefully, her stomach growling exuberantly at the thought of meat and spices and golden, delicious pastry crust.

West paused a moment, his eyebrow quirked in amusement over the loud, grumbling sound coming from her middle. "Two of 'em."

Bless him. "You're all right, O'Connell."

"Don't go telling anybody."

"Won't hear it from my lips," Sadie replied around a grin, and stepped over the threshold. Enveloped immediately by the hum of conversation buzzing around her, she walked a few paces, feeling more at ease than she had in hours. "Crowded," she commented, pleased for West's coin purse.

"Is," was the American's perfunctory response.

One corner of Sadie's mouth twitched up in a smirk at his curt reply. She started to say something tart back, but then she spotted a man across the tavern in subtly masculine hues and quality tailoring and swore under her breath instead. "What in devil's bollocks is *he* doing here?"

"Which 'he' are you referring to?" West inquired as he stepped alongside her. "There's a pub full of 'em." He tipped his chin toward the room filled with occupied tables.

"Castlebury," she ground out between her teeth, the very sight of the highborn toff setting her on edge. Too polished, too masculine, too handsome... too, well, simply *too*. Her gaze slipped down the front of his very fine breeches to the bulge she discovered there, but she quickly flicked it away as her cheeks flamed hot. Yes, *too*. Very much too.

Too intriguing to resist, her mind whispered.

Sadie's spine snapped straight as instant denial flooded her. "Watch me," she growled under her breath, purposefully turning her face away from the new Earl of Castlebury. It galled her how difficult the action was to perform and maintain, how much the tug of him pulled at her like a string attached between them, compelling her to glance back and seek his gaze once more.

"You talking about Carenza's brother?" West pointed a thumb across the pub. "Crawford?"

"Shh!" Sadie said, hunching her shoulders and yanking her hat low over her brow. "He'll hear you!"

"And that's a problem why?" West raised a hand in casual greeting to Lord Castlebury. "He knows about Carenza."

"But he doesn't know about me!" Sadie spat, darting behind a thick wooden support beam, lying to herself that she was slender enough to disappear behind it. Short she was, tiny she was not. Peeking at the earl from around the corner of the post, she added to West, "You don't know me, either."

Both of West's eyebrows shot up his forehead in surprise. "I don't?"

"No!" she whispered roughly. "You don't know Sadie Crisp." She frantically waved off the bartender and snuck another peek at Castlebury, noting his ice-fire eyes scanning the large room. "Now hush and don't ask questions." Sadie groaned and closed her eyes briefly. "Damnation, he's coming this way." Wiping suddenly sweaty palms over the thighs of her trousers, she inhaled a breath, hating how it hitched in her chest over the way Castlebury moved, all steady confidence and Corinthian strength.

Heart pounding, Sadie looked around desperately for an exit and found none. "Bollocks."

"Evening, gentlemen."

Sadie blanched at the sound of Castlebury's deep, cultured voice. She could not do this. If the earl discovered her truth, she could lose everything! Her job, her livelihood—her pocket-sized flat above the haberdashery. Good God, her *safety*.

"No," she whispered, and straightened away from the scarred wooden beam.

"Evening, Castlebury. What brings you by here tonight?" West asked, all amiability toward the earl.

"I was out for a stroll, contemplating how the illusion of something can appear as one thing, but in reality be another thing entirely. A curious encounter today has that conundrum occupying my thoughts. Sorting through it as I walked, I looked up and found myself on the doorstep of the Meadowlark, far from where I first began."

Alarm flashed bright in her head, blinding Sadie. Forgetting herself and her deal porter persona, she gasped and pushed clumsily away from the post and West. "Excuse me!" she squeaked.

"Why, Mr. Baker, is that you?" the earl asked, a false note of surprise ringing in his tone. A note that suggested that he was, in fact, not shocked at all that it was her. "Leaving so soon?"

Sadie darted for the heavy wooden door leading to the back.

"Mr. Baker?" West echoed back to Castlebury, sounding confused.

"Oh, shite," Sadie swore, and dashed over the threshold, fear skittering over her flesh. This was it. She knew it, just bloody *knew* it. The Earl of Castlebury was *it*.

He was the beginning of her end.

CHAPTER FIVE

CRAWFORD STOOD IN the middle of his office at Warehouse No. 3 on Tuesday morning with a cup of coffee strong enough to wake the dead, consternation twisting his mouth into a grimace. "How in devil's name am I supposed to even know where to bloody begin with all of this?" Weeks dedicated to untangling his father's personal ledgers well enough to deduce the state of the family's finances had left him little to no spare time to attend to Castle Shipping's own ledgers beyond the oddities he'd already noted. His mother's delicate state of grief, and caring for his youngest sister through the painful transition of losing their father, had kept him from his responsibilities at the docklands.

Fortunately, there had been Dobbs to manage things.

Unfortunately, there was no longer Dobbs.

"Bugger." Crawford sipped his coffee, uncaring at the sharply bitter note at the back of his tongue. That he had managed to make the cup of coffee with his own two hands was a near-miracle. A fine layer of grounds and an aroma of burned beans consisted of a victory to him. Even if he would be picking black bits from between his teeth all day. That was the least of his concerns.

Who can assist me with the running of this place? Someone with a sharp mind for numbers and organization, preferably.

"All a go, milord?" Woodmill poked his shaggy head through

the doorway, his deeply tanned face alight with goodwill and humor. "Piss hot today, ain't it?" He wiped a bead of sweat from his temple, grinning wide, and gestured to Crawford's attire. "Too much for the yard, all tha' finery. She's damper than a doxy's quim out there."

"Jesus," Crawford muttered, forcing that vivid imagery from his mind. "Message received." Grabbing his cravat, he yanked at the starched fabric, a part of him thrilling at the deconstruction of civility and social propriety with every knot he loosened. "I'll divest myself of a few items and we'll be off."

"Excellent!" the dockworker replied pleasantly, crossing his ankles as he relaxed and leaned against the doorframe, his shirt sleeves already rolled to his elbows. "Days like this, porters strip off tunics and haul in vests. Too bloody steamy to do else-wise."

Suddenly Crawford's mind filled with an image of big green eyes and feminine curves tucked inside a men's vest. "Well, let's go, shall we?" Amazing how quickly his waistcoat and jacket removed themselves! "Time's wasting." All that twisting and bending that Baker must be doing. All that heavy lifting with boards dampened by the moist heat. Surely Crawford was doing due diligence ensuring she didn't slip and fall on such a humid day, yes?

"Course, milord." Woodmill pushed away from the doorframe, his demeanor turning to business. "Sculler is waitin' quayside."

A slight hitch in Crawford's step was the only outward hesitation he displayed over climbing aboard the small vessel again. "No recent shark sightings?" he asked. Only to be thorough. An employer looked out for his employees, yes?

"None." Woodmill held up a hand, shaping his fingers into a zero as he led the way down the hall and out to the quay.

"Excellent!" Crawford said, instantly feeling foolish for his worry, following slowly behind.

Hopefully, the day would improve.

He held that hope even though Woodmill turned out to be

spot-on. It *was* damp on the docks. Perhaps not quite to the degree the dockworker had so eloquently described, but blasted humid, nonetheless. Crawford wiped at a trail of sweat trickling down the back of his neck and watched the controlled chaos of Surrey Commercial Docks working at full force. Lightermen and deal porters and dockworkers of all kinds moved in a type of coordinated dance, loading and unloading goods designed to satisfy the citizens of London and far beyond.

Crawford surveyed it all, soaking it in.

The rhythmic hustle and bustle of the docks was both mesmerizing and chaotic, a symphony of activity that seemed to dance before Crawford's eyes. He watched with a mixture of admiration and concern, his mind racing with thoughts of the responsibilities that lay heavy on his shoulders.

As he made his way through the maze of crates and barrels, he couldn't help but feel a sense of pride at the sight of Castle Shipping's operations in full swing. Despite the challenges he faced in managing the company's affairs, there was a certain satisfaction in knowing that he played a vital role in keeping the wheels of commerce turning. But amidst the organized chaos of the docks, there lingered a nagging sense of unease. The recent upheaval in his personal life had left him feeling unsettled, his thoughts consumed by worries about the future of his family's business and the safety of those under his employ.

Lost in his thoughts, Crawford barely noticed the approach of one of his foremen, a burly man with a weather-beaten face and a no-nonsense demeanor.

"Begging your pardon, milord," the foreman said, his voice gruff but respectful. "We've run into a bit of a snag with the loading of the cargo bound for Bristol. Seems there's been a mix-up with the manifests."

Crawford frowned, his brow furrowing with concern. "What sort of mix-up?" he asked, his mind already racing to find a solution to the problem.

The foreman shifted uncomfortably, his eyes darting around

as if he were afraid of being overheard. "Well, it seems that some of the crates were mislabeled, milord. We've already sorted out the ones that were meant for London, but it's going to take some time to straighten out the rest."

Crawford sighed, the weight of the situation settling heavily on his shoulders. "Very well," he replied, his voice firm with resolve. "We can't afford any delays, especially not now. Inform the porters to prioritize the correct crates and ensure that everything is properly accounted for."

The foreman nodded, his expression reflecting the seriousness of the task at hand. "Right away, milord. We'll have it sorted out in no time."

As the foreman hurried off to relay the orders, Crawford remained on the docks, his mind buzzing with plans and contingencies. Despite the challenges that lay ahead, he refused to let doubt or uncertainty cloud his judgment anymore. With new determination burning bright in his eyes, he set about the task of ensuring that Castle Shipping continued to thrive, no matter the obstacles that stood in his way. And as he surveyed the bustling activity of the docks once more, Crawford felt a glimmer of hope stirring within him. Despite the trials and tribulations that undoubtedly lay ahead of him, he was getting it sorted out. He had to believe that.

A splash sounded nearby, and Crawford's gaze flickered warily towards the murky waters of the Thames just beyond the bustling docks, his stomach churning uneasily at the memory of Dobbs's tragic fate. Despite the assurance that there had been no recent shark sightings, he couldn't shake the fear that lingered like a specter in the back of his mind. He swallowed hard, scanning the choppy surface of the river with a mix of trepidation and disbelief. The idea of a shark lurking beneath the murky depths seemed absurd, yet the memory of Dobbs being dragged beneath the surface by some unseen predator was enough to send a shiver down his spine.

"Pull yourself together, Crawford," he muttered, trying to

quell the rising tide of panic threatening to grip him. "There's no shark out there. It's all in your head." But try as he might to rationalize away his fear, the image of a dorsal fin slicing through the water refused to be dismissed. He couldn't shake the feeling of vulnerability that washed over him, the nagging worry that he was little more than prey waiting to be devoured.

"Christ, it probably has babies or a family or husband or what have you," he muttered darkly, his imagination running wild with vivid and unsettling scenarios. "And I'm not ripe for the eating. No thank you."

With a shake of his head, Crawford forced himself to tear his gaze away from the river, steeling himself. He had responsibilities to attend to, duties that required his full attention and focus.

Taking a deep breath to steady his nerves, he turned back toward the docks, his jaw set with determination. Despite the vague feeling of danger that hung over him like a cloud, he refused to be cowed… much.

⟫⟫⟫⟦⟦⟦

"FIVE STACKS OF five each, Palmer—I keep telling you that. It works best with five stacks of five each. Load gets uneven and unstable, you go any bigger than that. Deuce it, you've seen my sketched diagrams."

"Confuses me."

"Then listen to what I tell you and it'll work out just fine. I worked out the angles and strategy already."

"Ye're a quick 'un, Baker."

"Nah, just correct," the deal porter replied. "It's my curse."

Crawford's gut tightened with sudden awareness when he caught the womanly note in Baker's tone as he observed the dockside progress. How did everyone else miss it? Christ's sake, it was *right there*. He should know—he had been listening avidly to it since his arrival at Canada Yard almost an hour ago. The cadence, the undercurrent of breeding he could swear he detected…

Wait a moment, those lovely sounds coming from her mouth had formed words. What were they again?

Angles and strategy.

Crawford's gaze sharpened to a knife's point on the deal porter known as Baker, noticing everything about her at once: the tight, fit form tucked into loose-fitting men's clothing. At first her curves went unnoticed, but when she began to move over the planks, the roundness of her hips and plumpness of her backside became apparent. And when she bent to deliver the timber to its destination, an enticingly female indentation of waist flaunted itself for the briefest moment.

"Sweet Christ," he breathed, his desire fueled riotously to life by that seductive dip of waist, hidden from the world in plain view. Oh, what he could do with that gorgeous dip of femininity, how his lips could learn its every nuance and taste. Tonight, and every night going forward, it could own his fantasies.

Baker bent over and retrieved a pair of gloves from a pile of cut-and-prepped planks, her surprisingly full and shapely arse exposed by the tightening of her brown trousers across her backside. Crawford groaned softly, his own trousers going snug across the front. Embarrassment flooded him when he realized he had indeed groaned aloud… in public…

"Baker!" he called out, his voice hoarse. Clearing his throat, he called again. Why? Good blasted question. Crawford had no bloody idea. Outside of the lust hammering at him in the least gentlemanlike manner, nothing crossed his mind. It brimmed rather full of the image of an arse ripe and juicy enough to devour like a perfect, sun-kissed peach, lapping greedily at its sweet nectar.

What the deuce was he thinking?

"You're a blasted earl, for Christ's sake!" he muttered fiercely, clenching his hands into fists at his sides.

His gaze cared very little for his declaration, greedily seeking

Baker's backside once more as she shimmied her way down the lumber stack toward him. It killed him that she climbed down directly above him, giving his traitorous, libertine gaze a direct view of her secret delights.

"You are a gentleman," he scolded himself.

Baker spread her legs, searching with a booted foot for leverage on a jutting length of pine, and Crawford suddenly found himself staring at the apex between her thighs. It shocked him how fiercely he wanted nothing more than to undo the stitching at her trouser seam there with his teeth.

"A *gentleman*," he growled to himself, growing hot and aroused and appalled at his primitive reactions all at the same time. But damned if there wasn't something seductive as hell about a woman's shape shown off by a pair of trousers.

Suddenly, she was there in his mind again—only this time bare-breasted in only a pair of trousers—and Crawford's knees went weak. Good God, his mind today! Positively heathen.

"You called for me?"

Crawford blinked, focusing his attention. And there she was, standing directly in front of him in dockworker's clothing and a tatty cap, her green eyes impossibly wide and wary, a stray tendril of dark brown hair escaping to dance about her left ear. Without thought, he reached for it, rubbing the satin strands slowly between his fingers. "Soft," he murmured, his brain in such a fog-laden daze that he knew not what he was about. Her eyes, they… they *intoxicated* him.

"What do you want, Castlebury?" Baker jerked away from his touch, eyes going cold and shuttered.

Part of his brain registered the warning. But the other part— the part still floating like a lad after his first prigging—did not heed caution. Unfortunately, that portion connected to his mouth. "Come work for me in my office."

Baker tipped her head to the side as she looked up at him and seemed to consider. "Why would I do that?" she asked evenly.

"Better pay, less physical labor, and more suited to your skill with arithmetic and order," Crawford listed off. Just a few items that came to mind.

"Again"—she narrowed those incredible eyes on him, and his stomach quivered excitedly—"why would I do that?"

"Because I need a new Dobbs."

"And…?" Baker drawled, and slapped her hands on her waist—a decidedly female action. Were all the men at his bloody dock blind?

He leaned forward and whispered, "I know your secret. It's only a matter of time before they realize it too." Crawford hooked a thumb over his shoulder at the other deal porters.

Baker went utterly still. "What secret? I don't have a secret."

"Women aren't allowed to work on the docks. It's illegal and a punishable offense."

"I—" Baker said, those bewitching eyes of hers flashing with fear.

"Are obviously a woman in hiding," Crawford interjected, staring down at her, his brain consumed by this sudden, insatiable need to have her close to him. "And I can protect you if you come work for me in my office."

CHAPTER SIX

"Can you *believe* your brother? The audacity of the man!" Sadie flopped onto the closest piece of furniture, a cushioned settee of a rich golden hue in the drawing room of her best friend Lady Carenza Crowe's Belgravia townhome. "However did you survive your childhood with him and your father in charge? Ugh!" She punched a goose-down throw pillow. "Domineering oaf!"

"I cannot disagree, dearest," Carenza sympathized, turning from the window to pat Sadie's shoulder gently in understanding. "As the eldest Castlebury sibling, he aggravated me to no end with his overbearing manner. Always telling me what to do, so certain he knew the correct way. I think the heir apparent of a family is taught from the cradle of their most superior station—even amongst their own relations—and to never question themselves or their actions. Though Crawford is better than most, he still suffers from the condition, I'm afraid. The pressure of assuming the title pushes out all but the hardest of qualities."

"He's not a wholly bad sort..." Sadie said, a twinge of guilt forcing the words out. "Just arrogant and entitled and presumptuous and—"

"An earl," Carenza finished, her blue eyes full of compassion.

"An earl," Sadie agreed with a surrendering slump of her shoulders. The toned muscles went pliant under her plain gray dress. "Why must he be that way?" So deuced inconvenient.

Ruined all her carefully made plans. Well… perhaps not *ruined.*

Or perhaps so. It was entirely too early to tell.

"Consequence of his upbringing, I'm afraid." Carenza smiled wryly, her golden curls illuminated around her head by the sunlight streaming through the window. "Our father held little tenderness for his offspring." Though she said it lightly, Sadie heard the sadness tucked underneath. "Crawford learned early and well to be unmovable and unemotional on the surface."

Sadie raised her head from the back of the settee and eyed her closest friend curiously. "And underneath?"

Carenza laughed, the sound at once beautifully melodic and somehow ominous. "That, my dearest, only Crawford knows."

Sadie couldn't help but wonder what lay beneath Crawford's stern façade, hidden in the depths of his heart. "He's a puzzle, that's for certain," she mused, a thoughtful furrow creasing her brow as she considered the enigma that was the Earl of Castlebury. "But a puzzle I accept I may never solve."

Her friend tilted her head, studying Sadie with a knowing gaze. "And do you wish to solve it, the mystery that is my brother?"

Sadie hesitated, her mind swirling with conflicting emotions. Crawford's aloofness both intrigued and frustrated her in equal measure. "I…I'm not sure," she admitted. "There are moments when I find myself wishing to understand him, to peel back the layers and discover what lies beneath. But then there are times when I think it's best to leave well enough alone. Especially given my circumstances."

Carenza nodded in understanding, her expression sympathetic. "It's a delicate balance, to be sure. But perhaps it's not our place to unravel the mysteries of another's soul."

Sadie sighed, the weight of her own indecision pressing upon her. "Perhaps you're right," she conceded, sinking deeper into the cushions of the settee. "But it's hard to ignore the curiosity that gnaws at me, urging me to uncover the truth."

Placing a comforting hand on her arm, Carenza offered silent solace. "Whatever you choose, my dear, know that I will stand by your side. Whether you decide to delve deeper into the secrets of my brother's heart or to let them remain untouched, I'll support you."

Sadie offered her friend a grateful smile, touched by her unwavering loyalty. "Your friendship means more to me than words can express."

"Oh, I'm angling shamelessly for you to become my sister-in-law. It's all self-serving, believe me!" the viscountess confessed on a laugh.

"I'll take it anyway." Sadie grinned.

The two women shared a moment of lightness as the sun bathed the room in a warm, golden glow, casting long shadows that danced across the polished wooden floor.

As Sadie gazed out of the bay window, her mind wandered back to Crawford, the man who had disrupted her carefully laid plans. Despite his flaws, there was something undeniably compelling about him, something that drew her in despite her better judgment and the fact that she had no future and nothing to offer. Still… perhaps there was more to Crawford than met the eye. And perhaps, just perhaps, she was willing to risk uncovering the truth, whatever it may be.

Or maybe not, considering.

Ugh!

"Sadie, my dearest friend and confidante, I simply cannot bear to see you cooped up indoors and unhappy any longer," Carenza declared, her eyes sparkling with mischief as she clasped Sadie's hands in her own. "You need a break from all this worry and hiding. A breath of fresh air, a taste of the delights London has to offer."

Sadie's lips formed a tight line. "But you know Cousin Archibald is still hunting for me," she protested, her voice tinged with anxiety. "If he were to find me—"

Carenza waved away her worries with a dismissive flick of her wrist. "Nonsense, darling! We'll take every precaution necessary. You'll simply accompany me as my chaperone, or perhaps a companion. No one will give you a second glance in your modest attire."

Sadie hesitated. The threat of Cousin Archibald loomed large in her mind, casting a shadow over any semblance of peace or freedom. And yet a part of her longed for the chance to escape, even if just for a fleeting moment. "But what if something goes wrong?" Sadie asked, her voice quavering at the end. "What if he finds me?"

Carenza's expression softened, her gaze filled with unwavering determination. "We'll cross that bridge if we come to it. But for now, let's focus on the present. Let's seize the opportunity to enjoy a lovely afternoon together, just you and me."

A flicker of uncertainty passed through Sadie, but she couldn't deny the longing in her heart for a taste of freedom, for a reprieve from the constant fear that had plagued her since Cousin Archibald's treachery had been revealed. With a sigh, she relented, her shoulders sagging in defeat. "Very well," she acquiesced, her voice resigned but tinged with a hint of anticipation. "I do so miss modiste shops and French fabrics. But we must be cautious. I cannot afford to be reckless, not with my life at stake."

Her friend's eyes glowed with excitement, her smile brightening the room as she pulled Sadie into a tight embrace. "Of course, my dear. I'll keep a close eye on you, I promise. Now, let's not waste another moment. There's a delightful little tea shop on Bond Street that serves the most exquisite biscuits. I insist we pay it a visit."

And with that, the two friends set off, their laughter echoing through the corridors of Lady Carenza's Belgravia townhome. As they stepped out into the bustling streets of London, Sadie couldn't help but feel a flutter of excitement in her chest, a glimmer of hope amidst the shadows of fear and uncertainty. Perhaps, just perhaps, this would be the respite she so desperately needed.

The sun showered the cobbled streets of London as Sadie made her way with Carenza to the tea shop on Bond Street. Despite the lingering worry gnawing at Sadie's mind, she couldn't help but be captivated by the vibrant energy of the city. Oh, how she missed this part of London.

Someday. Someday I'll be back for real.

As they approached the quaint little tea shop, Sadie's eyes widened in wonder at the sight of the colorful displays of pastries and delicate china in the window. The tantalizing aroma of freshly brewed tea beckoned to her, coaxing a smile to her lips. "This looks glorious," she whispered excitedly.

Carenza led the way inside, with the gentle tinkling of a bell announcing their arrival. The interior of the tea shop was cozy and inviting, with plush armchairs arranged around small tables adorned with crisp white tablecloths.

A friendly-faced server greeted them with a warm smile, her eyes twinkling with mirth. "Welcome, ladies! What can I get for you today?"

The viscountess beamed at the server, her enthusiasm infectious. "Two pots of your finest tea, please, and a selection of your most delectable biscuits."

As they settled into their seats, Sadie felt a sense of peace slip over her. Surrounded by the comforting aroma of tea and the warm glow of friendship, she allowed herself to momentarily forget the troubles that had plagued her for so long. Allowed herself to believe for the briefest moment that she was once again Sadie Windcrisp, newly titled Duchess of Seawell.

Carenza poured them each a cup of tea, her movements graceful and precise. "Here's to a lovely afternoon spent in good company," she declared, raising her cup in a toast.

Sadie smiled, her heart swelling with gratitude for her steadfast friend. "To good company," she echoed, clinking her cup against Carenza's before taking a delicate sip. The worries that had consumed her seemed to fade into the background as she savored the simple pleasure of a warm cup of tea and the laughter of her dearest friend.

For a while, they lost themselves in conversation, sharing stories and reminiscing about happier times. Sadie found herself laughing more freely than she had in weeks, the heaviness that had settled in her chest lifting with each passing moment.

As they enjoyed their tea and biscuits, a pang of sadness hit her at the thought of returning to the reality of her hidden existence. But she also felt a newfound sense of strength and resilience, bolstered by the spontaneous outing.

With a sigh, Sadie straightened in her seat, feeling a renewed determination coursing through her veins. "Thank you, Carenza," she said, her voice soft but filled with sincerity. "For everything."

Her friend smiled, her blue eyes shining with affection. "Anytime, my dear. Remember, no matter what happens, you're not alone. I'll always be here for you."

Despite the pleasant distraction of the tea shop, a nagging worry tugged once more at Sadie's mind. "I really should not be seen out and about like this, and have probably pressed my fortune," she said, glancing around. "Cousin Archibald is still searching for me, and if he were to find me—"

"I understand your concerns." The viscountess smiled gently. "What about a quick stroll through Hyde Park to wrap up this lovely day?"

Sadie chewed on her bottom lip, torn between her desire for a moment of freedom and the fear of being discovered. But as she looked into Carenza's earnest gaze, she found herself slowly relenting. "I suppose a brief outing through Hyde Park to stretch our legs couldn't hurt," she conceded. "But we must be cautious, Carenza. I can't afford to be careless, not with Cousin Archibald on the prowl." She omitted the part about how he was searching for her alter ego now too. No need for everyone to fret—just her. It was *her* problem to remedy, after all.

Carenza squeezed her hand gently. "Don't worry—if anything should go amiss, we'll make a swift exit, just like we always do. And between your ferocious right cross and my healthy lung capacity for screaming, we'll be quite fine. I'm certain of it."

With a deep breath, Sadie nodded. "Very well, then," she said, her voice steadier now. "Let's make the most of this little excursion, shall we?"

Carenza's face lit up with a radiant smile. "That's the spirit! Now, let's enjoy the rest of our tea and biscuits before they get cold."

As they sipped their tea and indulged in the assortment of biscuits, Sadie felt the weight of her worries begin to lift again. But even as she savored the tranquility of the moment, she knew that their respite would soon come to an end.

As she and Carenza left the tea shop and strolled their way through Hyde Park, the lush greenery and serene atmosphere of the park provided a welcome respite from the chaos of London Society. The gentle rustle of leaves in the breeze and the distant murmur of conversation created a soothing backdrop to their conversation.

"It's been so long since I've indulged in the frivolous nonsense of *ton* events," Sadie remarked with a wistful smile, her eyes tracing the elegant lines of the park's pathways. "I never thought I'd miss it, but now it all seems so distant and surreal."

Carenza nodded in understanding, sweeping her gaze over the clusters of picnickers and leisurely strollers scattered throughout the park. "Indeed. After everything you've been through, it's no wonder you've come to appreciate the simplicity of a quiet walk in the park."

Sadie breathed in the fresh scent of grass and flowers, reveling in the sensation of sunlight warming her skin. For so long, she had been forced to live in the shadows, constantly vigilant against the looming threat of her cousin's treachery. But here, in the heart of Hyde Park, surrounded by the beauty of nature and the company of her dearest friend, she felt at ease.

As they continued their leisurely stroll, Sadie found herself drawn into the effortless rhythm of conversation, gossiping about the latest scandals and intrigues of London Society. Despite herself, she couldn't help but be amused by the absurdity of it all—the petty rivalries, the extravagant displays of wealth, and the elaborate social rituals that once seemed so important. It was as if a veil had been lifted from Sadie's eyes, allowing her to see the absurdity of it all with newfound clarity.

"It's all so... ridiculous, isn't it?" she remarked, a hint of amusement lacing her words as she observed a group of overdressed ladies vying for attention nearby. "The lengths people will go to for the sake of appearances."

Carenza chuckled softly. "But therein lies the charm of it all, does it not? The grand spectacle of Society, with its eccentric characters and elaborate masquerades."

Sadie couldn't help but laugh, her spirits lifted by the infectious joy of her friend. It was true—the world of the *ton* may be frivolous and absurd, but it was also undeniably captivating in its own way. And she missed it, blast it all.

As she meandered along the smaller path with Carenza, the scent of fresh earth and blooming flowers enveloped them. Sunlight filtered through the canopy of trees, casting dappled shadows on the ground below. The distant sound of laughter and chatter floated through the air, mingling with the gentle rustle of leaves.

"It's been ages since we've had a chance to simply stroll like this, hasn't it? Just the two of us out in the open." Carenza said as she glanced around at their surroundings.

Sadie nodded. "Indeed, it has. Not since before my parents passed. And I must confess, I've missed it more than I realized," she admitted, her gaze drifting over the tranquil scene before them.

"I daresay, I've missed sharing the latest gossip with you just as much. There's nothing quite like a scandalous tale to liven up the day."

She laughed in agreement, the sound echoing through the quiet surroundings. "You always did have a knack for finding the juiciest gossip," she teased, nudging Carenza playfully as they walked.

As they continued their stroll, they found themselves drawing closer to the edge of the woods, where the tranquil waters of the Serpentine glistened in the sunlight. The air was alive with the sound of birdsong, and a gentle breeze ruffled their hair as they walked.

"So, tell me, friend," Sadie began, her curiosity piqued. "What scandalous tales have you uncovered lately? Apparently, I'm positively itching to hear all the latest gossip."

Carenza leaned in conspiratorially, as if about to share the most scandalous secret. "Oh, where do I even begin?" she exclaimed. "There's talk of a certain marchioness caught in a compromising situation with a dashing young rake at Lady Doyle's soirée. And let's not forget the torrid affair brewing between Lord Montague and the vicar's daughter at his country estate!"

Sadie gasped dramatically, her hand flying to her chest in mock shock. "Goodness gracious, the *ton* is positively ripe with scandal!" she said, unable to suppress a giggle. "I must admit, I've missed the nonsense and frivolity of it all."

Carenza grinned, her laughter echoing through the quiet glade. "Ah, but that's what makes life in the *ton* so delightful," she replied. "Amidst all the chaos and lewdness, there's always something to entertain and amuse us."

As they reached the edge of the woods, the tranquil waters of the Serpentine stretching out before them, Sadie couldn't help but feel grateful for moments like these, moments of respite in a world filled with chaos and uncertainty. "I appreciate your talking me into this."

"Of course!" Her friend hugged her fiercely. "You needed it."

Suddenly, Sadie's heart lurched in her chest as she caught sight of the two men rounding the bend up near the edge of the forest. Instantly, she recognized the unmistakable figure of Cousin Archibald, his imposing frame cutting through the peaceful ambience of the park like a dark shadow.

Without a second thought, she abandoned Carenza's side, her breath catching in her throat as panic surged through her veins. With swift, determined strides, she dashed behind the nearest tree, her heart pounding in her ears. "Carenza, quickly!" she said, beckoning her friend to follow.

The urgency in her voice left no room for hesitation, and the viscountess, clearly sensing the gravity of the situation, hastened to join her behind the concealing foliage. "What is it?" Carenza asked, her eyes wide with concern as she peered past the tree trunk, trying to catch a glimpse of what had caused Sadie's sudden distress.

Sadie's breath came in short, rapid gasps as she struggled to compose herself, her mind racing with fear and uncertainty. "It's Archibald," she whispered hoarsely. "He's here, in the park."

Her friend's eyes widened in alarm, understanding dawning in her expression. "Shite in a basket," she breathed, her voice barely audible over the rustle of leaves and distant chatter. "We mustn't let him see you. We must find a way to slip away unnoticed."

Sadie nodded, her jaw clenched with determination as she peered cautiously around the trunk of the tree, her heart hammering in her chest. With Archibald so close, every instinct screamed at her to flee, to disappear into the safety of the shadows and evade his relentless pursuit.

As they watched from their hiding place, Sadie's heart sank further as she saw Archibald and his companion drawing nearer, their conversation drifting on the breeze. She could feel the weight of his presence like a leaden anchor, threatening to drag her down into the depths of despair.

"We must find another way out of the park," she whispered, her voice tinged with desperation. "We cannot risk being seen."

Carenza nodded in agreement, scanning their surroundings for any sign of escape. "There's a path just beyond those bushes," she murmured, gesturing toward a thicket of foliage nearby. "If we can make it there without being seen, we may be able to slip away unnoticed."

Sadie's heart thumped erratically as she prepared to make a run for it. With one last glance at Archibald and his companion, she braced herself for the mad dash ahead.

"Ready?" Carenza whispered, clasping Sadie's hand in a gesture of solidarity.

Sadie nodded, her resolve hardening as she steeled herself for what lay ahead. With a silent prayer on her lips, she took a deep breath and bolted from their hiding place, her senses attuned to every sound, every movement, as she raced toward the safety of the bushes. "Go, go, go!"

As they reached the cover of the foliage, Sadie spared a fleeting glance over her shoulder, her heart pounding a maddening pace in her chest. To her relief, she saw no sign of Archibald or his companion, their presence fading into the distance like a nightmare slowly receding with the dawn. With a sigh of relief, she allowed herself to slump against the trunk of a nearby tree, her chest heaving with exertion and relief.

Beside her, Carenza placed a comforting hand on her shoulder. "We made it," her friend said softly, her voice filled with relief. "You're safe now."

"Thank you," Sadie replied, her voice feeling almost raw in her throat. "I don't know what I would do without you."

Carenza smiled warmly. "When the Revivalists came to the tavern and nearly killed you and West because of Lord Arnold's sick need for me, you were there. You got hurt protecting me. We're in this together, come what may."

True friends were everything.

"Well," Sadie said, brushing bits of leaves and twigs from the front of her dress as her heart overflowed, "this turned out to be quite the eventful tea and biscuit outing after all."

Carenza raised a golden eyebrow and laughed, linking her arm through Sadie's as they made their way back to the viscountess's townhome. "With us, is there any other kind?"

CHAPTER SEVEN

C RAWFORD DREADED FAMILY dinner night. Not usually, and not in general, but tonight he was making an exception. "There will be *no* wife hunting."

No hunting, no list, no discussion. Nothing at all. He had decided upon it. As the head of the Castlebury family, he ought to be able to make such a proclamation and expect it to be executed exactly so.

Not in his family.

"Oh, Crawford dearest!" his mother cried over the dinner table, directing his attention to her with a slight tip of her head into his line of vision. Her smile rang false to him, forced. Whether from the strain of family dinner while still grieving her husband or from her perpetual frustration with Crawford's lack of enthusiasm for a wife hunt, he hadn't the faintest notion. Whatever the cause, her smile looked brittle enough to shatter. "Have you been much acquainted with the Marquess of Lyondale and his marchioness?"

Bloody hell, his mother was relentless. Clearing his throat, he reached for his glass of wine and managed a slightly desperate swallow.

"Well, do you?"

Crawford held up an index finger in a silent bid for her to stand by, wishing fervently for a larger glass filled with a *lot* more wine, gulping it down like a fish stranded and flopping on a riverbank.

"For goodness' sake," Lady Castlebury grumbled, waiting for him to finish. Her fingers impatiently drummed the polished tabletop, outward evidence of her vexation.

"I'm afraid…" he began in a vaguely panicked tone, looking around at his siblings for assistance and finding none. *Blackguards.* "I'm afraid that I am not much acquainted with them, Mother."

She leapt. Like a fox on a field mouse. "Oh, lovely!" Her smile broadened into one full of sincere eagerness. "I shall make introductions, then! They've a wonderful estate in Berkshire teeming with the plumpest fowl. Oh yes, you *must* meet them."

"The marquess or the fowl?" he couldn't help but ask.

"The marquess and his lady, of course! Absolutely delightful they are. So very respectable, and with impeccable breeding, I must confess."

They've a daughter of…

He waited for it.

One heartbeat.

Two.

"They've a daughter of particular talent with the cello. Quite the most engaging instrument, really, when played with modest decorum to the side as she does."

There it was.

"Have you had the pleasure of listening to the cello played with a feminine hand?"

Could he avoid answering and live to tell of it the next day? Crawford slid his mother a discreet glance, gauging her. Most decidedly not. "I, ahem, have not experienced such entertainment, I'm afraid." He knew as soon as the words were uttered that he was doomed.

"Oh, that is most fortunate, then!" Lady Castlebury beamed, her excitement barely contained. "The marquess is hosting a garden concert in the coming days, and we shall attend."

"But Mother," Lottie interrupted from her chair further down the table, "won't that be frowned upon? We *are* still in mourning." The youngest Castlebury speared her wedge of seasoned roast potato, a frown marring the space between her eyebrows.

"Indeed, we are," murmured their mother, a flash of sadness appearing in the depths of her eyes, quickly gone. She straightened and dabbed the corner of her mouth with a pristine fabric napkin before stating, "While we *are* in mourning and will continue to be so for the defined, appropriate amount of time, we also must continue with the details of estate business. One such detail is a match for Crawford as the new Earl of Castlebury and head of this family."

"Oh, for the love of Chr—" Crawford started, irritation flaring hot at the base of his neck.

"How is your play coming along, young playwright?" Rainville practically shouted from his seat near the middle of the table as he leaned over his plate to address Lottie, his golden gaze shooting warning darts at Crawford. "I am most eager to read it."

That was all the encouragement Lottie needed, and she launched into an impassioned, one-sided conversation about the merits of her latest revision of the third act, successfully cutting Crawford off and saving the table conversation from devolving into an argument. Knowing that he owed his new brother-in-law a thank you, Crawford gave a quick, almost imperceptible nod of appreciation for the duke's quick intervention. Noting it in his mind, he promised himself he'd send Rainville a bottle of brandy from his father's—no, now *his*—private collection.

"You know he esteems you greatly."

Turning his head to his right, Crawford leaned toward his sister Nora and replied, "He has a knack for assisting others during challenging situations."

His younger sister glanced at her husband, affection and humor ripe in her green eyes. "That he does, indeed."

"Speaking of situations…" Carenza piped up from the left side of their mother, her gaze bright and direct and filled with curiosity as she stared Crawford directly in the eye from diagonally across the table. "Am I correct in what I'm hearing, dear brother, about your management style down at the Commercial Docks?"

"Surrey Docks or all of the docks?" he instantly asked, wanting to pinpoint the gossip's origination point.

"Surrey. Why, are you behaving oddly at the London Docks as well?" His eldest sister propped her chin on her hand and leaned forward, gaze intent on him. "From what I've gleaned, your behavior has been highly erratic."

Crawford narrowed his eyes on his sister. "What exactly have you gleaned, and from whom?"

"I do quite emphatically believe I'm a more competent writer than Goodrich!" Lottie's voice rose above the others.

"And what, pray tell, makes you qualified to make such judgment?" This from Rainville as he reclined in his chair and hitched a sapphire-blue velvet-covered arm over the back, looking very much the showman duke as he challenged Lottie with a quirked bronze brow. "I've the theatre company."

"Only because you're a man," muttered Lottie as she stabbed at the vegetables on her plate.

"Oh ho!" called Rainville, grinning wildly.

"Do not encourage him, Lottie, I beg you," came from an exasperated Nora, her hand darting out to grasp her sister's in a white-knuckled fist.

"And what would you do, were Rhodes Theatre yours to have any way you chose?" The duke patted his wife's other hand and leaned into the lively debate, clearly loving it.

"Honestly?" Lottie sipped from her glass and considered. "I would employ a co-playwright for Goodrich. One who could offer advice and editing for his plays, one who held substance. Anyone afraid of your surly wordsmith would not do. It should be a person of courage and stability and soundness of mind, for I have oft wondered at the soundness of his."

"You've given Thatcher considerable thought," Rainville murmured, a considering look coming into this lionlike gaze. "Why is that, I wonder?"

"I've given his creative choices considerable thought, yes. That is true. But that is all." Lottie leveled a stubborn stare at Rainville. "Absolutely nothing more."

"What about you, Crawford? What choices are you affording thought to lately?"

Deuce it all, not his mother again.

Crawford eyed his fork and wondered briefly if self-inflicted pain was worth getting out of the rest of dinner for.

His mother would still undoubtedly henpeck him while he was infirm. So, no. Not worth it—though possibly the less agonizing choice. "They have mostly revolved around the financial health of the estate."

"Hmm." His mother set her napkin on the table beside her plate and masked her emotions perfectly. "And how is the health of the estate?"

"Robust," Crawford answered honestly as conversation buzzed all around the table.

"Excellent," she replied with a pleased smile, glancing around the table briefly. "It is good to know all is in order. As it is, shan't that provide you opportunity for other endeavors? Ones of a more personal nature?"

Feeling a roar of frustration rising inside him, Crawford drew a deep breath and took several moments to pause while he looked about the dining room, noting the rich peach-blossom wall color, the polished walnut furniture, the gilt-framed paintings of various English and French landscapes. "I've been considering a long trek through the north of Scotland," he admitted, stopping to admire an oil painting of Glen Nevis, riotous and wild with life in summer, the giant *ben* dominating the background. A long, *long* trek.

"That's not the sort of personal endeavor I'm referring to, Crawford Hunnewell Castlebury, and you well know it." All attempts to mask her vexation vanished. The countess glared at him outright and grumbled, "You are *extremely* trying to my nerves."

Guilt pricked him. Hard.

Damnation.

"I should," Crawford started, but his throat squeezed tight, and he sounded like a strangling man. He stopped to cough and gulp more wine. *Dear God, please don't punish me for what I am about to do. It was out of love. Love. Take pity on me.* "I, um, should…" Blast it, this was difficult. "I should be pleased to escort you to the marquess's garden concert."

His mother narrowed her eyes in suspicion. "To hear their daughter's gift with the cello?"

Crawford glanced to the ceiling and grasped for his rapidly diminishing patience. "Yes, to hear their daughter's cello."

"*Delightful!*" she exclaimed, clasping her hands together and beaming at him. "I am beyond pleased to finally be starting on my list!"

Shite.

"Mother, I didn't agree to start on your list." Panic fluttered to life in his belly, and he set his wine glass down, his appetite suddenly soured.

"You sort of did, actually," Lottie corrected him around a mouthful of asparagus on toast.

"I hate to say I agree with Lottie, but I must," Carenza's husband, Damon, said as he slipped stealthily into the room and sat down next to his wife. His dark gaze lit with humor as he smiled, showing off a crooked incisor. "And everyone knows that once you open the floodgates…"

"Nobody bloody asked you," Crawford growled at his brother-in-law, snatching a roll and taking a huge, ungentlemanly bite. Feeling defensive and not ready for a blasted wife hunt or marriage, no matter that he was supposed to be, he leaned far back in his seat at the head of the table and stretched his legs out in front of him. Crossing his ankles and arms, he created a fortress with his body, barring anyone from getting the idea that he welcomed further conversation. "Besides, you're late."

"Apologies on that. Assignment held me up." Damon flashed

a smile about as open and welcoming as a wolf's, his signal that the topic was to remain undiscussed.

"You're well?" Carenza instantly cupped her husband's cheek, concern misting her eyes. "Nothing broken?"

"Nothing of mine, *hechicera*," Damon said gently, cupping her chin in return. "Do not worry yourself." His dark head dropped to hers, and their foreheads touched briefly.

The obvious love and devotion between the two sent Crawford's mind careening into his emotions, resulting in a spontaneous and rather alarming flash of envy right in the center of his chest. "What the d—?" he began, cutting off when his heart bound tight and squeezed viciously. And suddenly there she was, the woman in trousers. Baker. Directly in the front of his mind, staring him down with challenging eyes of the most magnificent green. Calling to him like a selkie called to her lover. Secrets and mystery and danger entwined.

Irresistible, all of it.

"Bollocks and damn," he cursed, blinking hard and scrubbing a hand over his face. *No, no, no.* This was not happening. Not now, not ever.

"I say, Crawford, are you well?" his mother inquired with alarm in her tone.

"Fine," he croaked.

"Your tardiness had nothing to do with those awful Revivalists, did it?" Lottie asked Damon, blind to Crawford's distress. "I heard from Miss Lucinda Pines at the tea shop earlier today of their latest attack, and that there are still no leads. Catamount said as much himself only last week. It's dire indeed when the captain of the Bow Street Runners says such a thing," she added with a decisive nod. "You wouldn't be working on anything to do with them, would you?"

"No." Damon leveled his dark, unreadable gaze on Lottie. "I am not."

"Oh," Lottie replied, her shoulders slumping a little in relief. "I'm glad of it. Just Society secrets, then?"

"Hm," was all Damon replied.

"Stop questioning the man, young playwright. You'll only tire yourself and learn nothing. Trust me," Rainville drawled. "I've wasted more breath on that endeavor than I care to admit."

"No harm done when one is so very full of hot air. There's plenty of breath to spare." Damon's grin sliced wickedly across his face.

"Touché," the duke replied with a tip of his wine glass in Damon's direction.

Crawford had a sudden thought and cut his sister an assessing look. "Carenza, how is it that you seem to be privy to dockland gossip?"

"Oh, you know," his sister replied, dotting the corner of her mouth with a napkin. "I hear things here and there."

"But dockland gossip tends to stay within the docks," Crawford pressed, leaning forward and bracing his forearms on the table, his instincts jumping. "To hear it, one generally must know a person of the docks personally or be one themselves. Since you're clearly not a waterman… Who do you know?"

"Would you look at that bit of lamb! So delectable it appears! I'll have some."

"Carenza," he said in a quiet, low tone. What was she hiding? Or whom? "Who do you know down at the Commercial Docks?"

"Oh, Crawford dearest!" his mother interjected. "Did I mention that the marquess's daughter, Lady Emelina, is also an accomplished equestrian? I'm quite certain you'll find much to discuss at the garden concert. In fact, I'm sure we can arrange for the two of you to go riding together on a separate day."

Enough.

Scraping his chair back from the table, Crawford stood and stiffly inclined his head. "If you'll excuse me." He needed to escape.

"Where are you going, old chum?" The note of humor in Rainville's tone was not lost on him. The duke clearly understood his discomfort. Unsympathetic prat.

"I'm heading out!" Crawford called from the foyer.

"Out?" his mother's voice echoed back.

"Out!" Crawford grabbed his coat from the waiting footman and barely broke stride as he stepped through the front door. Bugger it if he knew where he was headed.

The only thing that mattered was that it wasn't Tipton House.

CHAPTER EIGHT

CRAWFORD WOKE THE next morning with a screaming cramp in his neck and the taste of soiled stockings in his mouth. "Wha—?" he garbled, swiping groggily at the corner of his mouth. Was it wet? Bollocks, had he been drooling? "Where 'm I?"

Wincing with pain, he struggled to sit up, grabbing at the muscle in his neck currently locked into the shape of a beach pebble and feeling every bit as hard. He grunted and pinched the spot with unforgiving fingers. "Fuck me Tuesday," he said between his teeth, and dropped back down to the sofa.

What a lovely way to begin the day.

"And they say a privileged life is an easy one." Feeling sorry for himself, Crawford dragged his body vertical and tried to take in his surroundings with gritty, tired eyes. His neck instantly protested with a spasm of searing intensity. Feet shooting out in front of him, ramrod straight, Crawford released a round of swearing foul enough to turn a pirate's head and latched on to his neck with both hands. Probably he deserved it for acting petulant and whining.

"How in the devil's lair were you able to even sit here?" he asked his father's memory as he rose stiffly from the sofa he knew well from his youth. Why Winslow Castlebury had insisted on keeping the hideously uncomfortable thing all these years, he never understood. "I will burn your cursed cushions with glee."

Glaring at the ugly brown offender, Crawford rubbed at the sore muscles and tried to remember how he'd gotten to the warehouse last eve to begin with. Fuzzy recollections of West pouring him into a hack from the back door of the Meadowlark Tavern surfaced, and then further ones of him directing the driver to Warehouse No. 3, North Quay, which actually made some sense. *Even foxed me doesn't want to be around my mother and her bloody list.*

Marriage. *Bleh.* How about giving him time to get his bearings as earl first? Perhaps others stepped into their titles with confidence and grace, but that seemed to be rather the opposite of how Crawford felt about his inheritance. As eldest he had always held position over his siblings, an expectation, a certain responsibility of behavior and sobriety of demeanor the others hadn't been groomed into as he had been. As a result, what he displayed on the outside often mismatched his feelings on the inside.

Right now, his insides wanted to heave.

Hastening to the large, multi-paned window, Crawford shoved the drapes wide open and grimaced his way through opening the sash. A blessedly cool early morning breeze swept his cheeks and calmed his quarrelsome stomach. Gulping Western Dock air like it was the freshest in England, he placed his palms on the thick windowsill and leaned through the opening, glancing down to see lamp glow abundant along the North Quay. Across the wide, still waters of the dock, he noted the sun only beginning to lift the blanket of darkness, the faintest blush of lavender whispering across the far horizon. Soon dawn would break, and the quay would bustle with workers. For now, a quiet peacefulness permeated Western Dock. Even the mighty ships making berth along her edges seemed content to float in silent sentry, guardians until their next voyage.

It was strangely… serene.

"Is this where you found your rest?" he wondered aloud, thinking of his father. Was that lumpy, godawful sofa and this place where Winslow Castlebury had finally been able to sleep? Crawford thought of the couch divots, the patterning to them, and the shape of the human form. "You crafty ol' bugger. I bet you only paced the gardens until Mother was certain to be asleep, and then you came here."

His father had found peace on the water.

"And here I thought I couldn't learn anything new about you." More fool him. Scrubbing a hand over his unshaven face, Crawford sighed heartily and tried to come back inside. The cravat he had apparently unknotted last night and left in dangled dishevelment about his neck caught on a protruding nail jutting from the window frame and nearly strangled him. Muttering every swear word he had learned at Eton—which was an impressive lot—Crawford fought a short, furious battle with the nail until the fine linen tore and the force of his yanking tossed him backward onto his arse on the hardwood floor.

"Damn my life!" he yelled, throwing the ruined cravat as far away from him as possible. It landed in a crumpled bundle behind his father's sofa, lost to the black beyond.

Of course.

Of bloody fucking course.

"I thought I heard noise in 'ere."

"Mr. Woodmill," Crawford begrudgingly greeted the man from his position on the floor, his back to the door. Embarrassment flushed his cheeks, heated them. How much had the dockworker overheard? "Apologies for the outburst. A momentary lapse in manners."

"Nuffin' of it, milord." Woodmill cheerfully waved him off, stepping into the enormous corner office. "Docks is worse. Lots."

And here Crawford thought his Eton swear vocabulary impressive. Next to dockworkers, it ranked about as salty as honey.

Was he vaguely disappointed?

Huh.

"I'll make coffee." Grunting with the effort, Crawford dragged his arse into standing position, flinching slightly at the tenderness in his right buttock. He refused to rub it and make a further fool of himself in front of his employee.

"No, no," the dockworker rushed to say. "I got it." He chuckled. "For bof our sakes. I smelled tha' shite of yours." Moving to the cabinet where the beans were stored, Woodmill went about prepping coffee. "Do this e'ery mornin' at me home."

"Say," Crawford said, having a thought. "Did you much come across my father here early in the morning like this?"

"Didn't." Woodmill shook his head, busy with his work. "Dobbs, though."

"Dobbs saw my father here early in the mornings?" Raking a hand through his tangled auburn strands, Crawford scanned his father's—no, *his*. Damn, why did he keep doing that?—office to Castle Shipping. Though he had stood in the same spot hundreds of times before, he saw it now with new eyes. Expensive, plush Persian rugs, gorgeous cabinetry obviously imported from the East Indies, gold-framed paintings of Greece and Constantinople and Rome. Glossy wooden model ships decorating the fireplace mantel. Maps unrolled and spread across a large, sturdy table, and held down with glass paperweights he recognized as West Indian design—all bold colors and palm leaves and tropical birds. Spyglasses, compasses, wooden vases of intricately carved East African patterns.

Well, he'd be damned. This, *this* was the real Winslow Castlebury.

World traveler. Collector. Shipping magnate.

"Most days, wot I heard." Woodmill handed him a steaming cup of brilliant-smelling coffee. "Dobbs 'spected it."

'Spected?

Expected. Ah, now he had it. "Continue," Crawford said, and tucked into the dark, rich brew. Woodmill's far exceeded his feeble attempt for taste and smell and veritably everything.

"Nuffin' more to tell, milord. Dobbs wot kept himself to himself most of'en."

"Thank you for the coffee," came out of Crawford on a wave

of gratitude as blessed alertness began to creep through him.

Woodmill grunted in acknowledgment and drank from his own cup, his hard workman's hands swallowing the fine porcelain. "Loads o' work today. Drink up an' I'll tell you."

How could Crawford tend to business with his mind still overcoming its sluggish beginnings? Perhaps another cup of Woodmill's coffee… "Care to make another round, ol' chum?" he asked hopefully.

Woodmill chuckled and nodded his agreement. "Tobacco shipment to unload at Surrey Docks today. Got Baker on lead with tha', though no' his usual haul. Wanted 'is smarts. *Blue Nellie* made port right afore I came in 'ere."

Baker.

"*Blue Nellie?*" Crawford asked, his heart rate increasing at Baker's name.

"Full-rigged ship. Five bloody huge masts wot square-rigged, stacked high as can spot wit' yer peepholes." Woodmill spread his arms wide in demonstration.

How about that? Crawford's mind was suddenly rather awake and eager to see this tobacco shipment. Never mind the many, *many* he had witnessed over the years.

This one was special. Because of the *Blue Nellie*, of course. He'd never seen one of its particular kind before. All the masts were *square*. Fascinating stuff.

Truly.

"Let's get to it, shall we?" Crawford turned with a newly acquired spring in his step, forgetting all about his need for more coffee. Suddenly he had plenty of energy.

"SHE'S A BEAUTY, she is." Woodmill puffed his chest with pride as he gestured to the massive ship's poop deck, which they currently stood upon. Hustle and bustle greeted them as workers hoisted rigging, swabbed the main deck, and hauled hogshead barrels of tobacco down the plank to waiting dock men ready to lighten their burdens. "Biggest lady e'er wot grace London Docks."

"I believe it." Winslow Castlebury had wanted the best of the best. Always. Fitting that he would have possessed the largest ship in the docklands. Anything to publicly display his success and poke at the East India Company. In his mind, Castle Shipping stood elbow to elbow with the powerful entity. While that wasn't exactly the case, Castle Shipping *did* boast the title of second largest and most influential shipping company in England. Which was damned impressive.

And Crawford's to run with at least equal success.

No pressure.

"Bloody sweltering out today," Crawford muttered, and tugged at his jacket collar with two fingers, providing space for blessed fresh air against the heated skin of his neck. He cast his pale gaze to the flurry of activity on the deck below and ignored the flutter of panic in his chest. Anyone would feel daunted at the magnitude of such an inheritance. An earldom alone was significant. Also inheriting the largest and most powerful shipping empire outside the East India Company moved it from significant to *holy shite.*

Crawford wasn't ashamed to admit that he felt that way.

At least to himself.

"Nah, she ain't sweltering. She's bare warm yet. Piss hot later, though."

"Christ, Woodmill." Crawford grimaced at the picture painted by the dockworker's words. "You've a way with verbal imagery, I'll give you that." Clasping his hands behind his back, he fought the urge to fiddle with the giant wheel below them on the quarterdeck, the child inside him excited to be standing aboard such a mighty vessel. As a young boy he had often thought a life of piracy would suit him. Anything to be unhindered and free.

"I'll show you more of *Blue Nellie.* Come." Woodmill gestured toward the stairs. "Af'er you, milord."

Once down the stairs and settled on the quarterdeck, Woodmill turned to the narrow set of intricately carved doors behind them that led to the captain's quarters. "Inside is sumfin' else."

"Woodmill, I got them crates! They been pried open like wot ye afeared!"

"Bugger," the dockworker said. "Comin'!" He turned his brown head and called out, "Baker, show the earl the captain's quarters!"

"What? Me? Why?" Baker instantly questioned, sounding suspicious and not entirely pleased with the order.

Crawford whipped his head up, his gaze seeking the form that had burned itself into his mind. When he found it down on the main deck, his body tensed at the sight of Baker's compact, feminine form barely hidden beneath loose trousers and a waistcoat. "Because I wish it," slipped from his lips before he was aware he'd even spoken. "And because Mr. Woodmill is needed elsewhere at the moment."

And because the thought of being alone with her was irresistible.

"Woodmill!" called the quayside dockworker again. "Tampered barrels!"

"Comin'!" Woodmill turned to Baker. "Show 'im inside."

"Fine," huffed the woman in disguise known as Baker. "Follow me."

Amused and intrigued at the forced huskiness in her voice, Crawford waited for her to brush past and murmured, "I'm all yours," simply to see what she would do.

Baker tripped over the threshold.

"Steady there." Reaching out, he latched on to a surprisingly firm and substantive upper arm, and drew Baker upright once more. Lips twitching over her response to his provocative words, he leaned down to her ear and added with humor ripe in his tone, "Careful that you don't give yourself away, *la petite femme*."

She glared at him, her magnificent emerald dagger eyes meant to slice and stab without mercy. "I am *not* a little lady," she spat from between her teeth.

His eyebrows shot up his forehead in surprise. *"Parlez-vous Francais?"* How did this little hideaway understand French?

Baker's eyes widened a fraction, and she looked around behind her at the busy ship deck and the dock men and sailors busy transferring the cargo to the solid footing of the quay. "I-I don't know what you just said," she stammered, and yanked her arm from his grip. "Let's get this over with."

Crawford's gaze drifted down her back and over her delectably round backside to her thighs—her delightfully *shapely* thighs. No skin-and-bones miss here. Oh no, Baker was all firmness and curves. An extremely delicious combination, it turned out.

Crawford's mind flashed an image of her succulent thighs wrapped tightly around him as he drove into her, relentless in his passion. *"Whoa,"* rushed from his lungs even as his gaze whipped straight back to her backside. He literally couldn't help it. It was the most gorgeously shaped arse he had ever seen.

I want to bite it.

What?

Hard.

Crawford froze in his tracks. *Beg pardon?*

I want to bite it hard enough to sting, and then I want to lick and nibble every bare inch of it until she's wet and begging for me.

"Are you coming?" Baker impatiently asked over her shoulder.

Good God, nearly.

"Yes!" Crawford croaked, his breeches straining across his swelling cock. Arousal swirled low in his belly, heated him. Jolting into motion, he hastened through the double doors and stepped into the captain's quarters of the *Blue Nellie*.

His footsteps faltered. "Wow." Just… wow.

It was like he had stepped inside a cave to a pirate's treasure room. Gold *everywhere*. His arousal dimmed as he stared transfixed at the sight before him.

"Bloody ridiculous, isn't it?" Baker snorted derisively, nudging a solid gold figurine on the floor next to her with a booted foot.

Crawford looked around with big eyes. "Are you certain…" he began slowly, taking in the blood-red velvet curtains, the gold filigree and inlaying, the jewel-encrusted swords and shields. The literal boxes of gold coins stacked one upon the other, from largest to smallest. "You're certain that this ship was not my father's favorite?" This showpiece seemed much more to his liking.

Baker shook her head, her frayed gray tweed cap wobbling with the motion. "*Susanna's Secret.* He was adamant about that." A stray strand of dark brown hair slipped loose from her workman's cap to flutter about her left cheek. Instantly, his gut tightened with the desire to see all of that hair she cleverly hid under her cap. He wanted it cascading down her back and sliding through his fingers. He wanted it wrapped in his fist while he thrust into her deep and long.

"I'm surprised," Crawford admitted, his voice rough, raising his hand to grasp the wayward strand gently, rubbing it slowly between his fingers. "Such lushness as this is hard for a man to resist."

Her eyes widened, but she did not pull away. Taking that as encouragement, he traced featherlight fingers across the line of her jaw, loving the silken feel. "I knew you would feel like this," he whispered. "Soft as spring blossoms." How was that possible for a woman working on the docks? Leaning forward, he inhaled her scent. Ocean breeze and fresh soap and an underlying warmth that was distinctly *her.* "Smell good too," he murmured, tenderly tipping her chin up and bringing her full, sensual lips to his.

Lights exploded behind his eyelids. Sparks and flashes and swirls.

When Crawford's lips touched hers, the world shifted and flooded with color. Magnificent, glorious color. It came alive.

He came alive.

"Good God, what *are* you?" he breathed, cupping her cheeks

in both his hands and pulling back just far enough to stare into her brilliant green eyes. "You're a selkie, that's what you are. Come to spellbind me."

"Oh!" she replied in a wholly feminine tone, her firm little body melting into his. "You think?" The way she said it, Crawford knew she rather liked the idea.

He took her mouth, kissed her hard. Teased her with his tongue along the seam of her lips, licking provocatively. "Selkie mine."

"Mm," she mewed, opening for him.

He thrust his tongue inside. "Careful I don't hide your coat, keep you for myself." A nip of her plump bottom lip. "Your name, Selkie. Give me your name."

"No," she moaned, wrapping her arms around his neck and meeting his tongue with a lush stroke of her own.

Crawford turned the kiss darker, hotter. "Name," he panted several minutes later. He thrust his thigh between her legs, rubbed her through her trousers. "Your real one."

"Damn it," she said, rocking into him. "You had to use those thighs." Gripping his neck tighter, she rocked again and moaned, going restless and wanting. "Oh, I like your thighs."

Noted, he thought wickedly. "Name." He rubbed his thigh against her core, felt her shiver. His mouth coaxed her with a slow, drugging kiss.

"Sadie Crisp," she whispered, and went boneless.

"Sadie," he breathed against her lips, liking the sound.

"Baker, quayside now, you lazy git! Work wot needs doin'!" The gravelly voice rang out sharp from just outside the captain's quarters.

The two of them jumped apart like their clothes were on fire, brushing and tugging and slapping at their outfits to right them before anyone noticed something amiss. Baker—no, *Sadie Crisp*— refused to look at him.

Christ, what lunacy had that just been?

A rap of knuckles against the door, and Woodmill poked his

head in. "We should ge' on, milord. Day's full yet."

Aaand that was that.

Crawford smiled at Woodmill and ignored the unspent arousal raging inside him, the churning emotions, the burning questions. Tonight, he predicted, would be a very long, highly frustrating night.

"Let us carry on, shall we?" He cleared his throat. "Thank you for the tour. Good day, Baker." He glanced back to nod farewell to the woman who fueled his fantasies.

But Baker was already gone.

CHAPTER NINE

"H E REALLY HAD no business kissing me," Sadie grumbled under her breath as she made her way home that evening after her shift at the docks. The sun hung low in the sky, glowing a rather unsettling shade of red through the haze of London's dirty air. It tinted everything scarlet. If she weren't so focused on the very real fact that the Earl of Castlebury had planted his lips on hers in a way that hadn't been wholly unacceptable, she might have noticed the ominous quiet of her surrounding and the lack of usual evening activity.

"I'll protest if he tries again."

She knew that for the lie it was the moment the words exited her mouth. It was rather likely she would tangle her tongue with his and kiss him back with equal fervor. Damn Castlebury and his tree-trunk thighs. They caused her good sense to up and desert her.

I am a damsel in distress, not a light-skirt searching for her next benefactor. Not that she remotely wanted to be that damsel in distress—and she *wouldn't* be if the laws were the slightest bit fair to women. English laws were made by men intent on keeping women meek and powerless.

And that is exactly why I live in the trade district in a flat the size of a boot box, hiding my very existence. It's either that or die. Sadie very much wished to *live.*

Bollocks to it all.

Crossing Wapping High Street, she caught sight of Tower Bridge off to her left, looming tall and imposing over the Thames in the growing dusk as she turned from the water and headed inland for the two-mile walk to Watling Street in Cheapside. Thirty minutes more and she would be home.

"I wonder if Frau Olsen has any soup left," she mused aloud, feeling her stomach growl, and spotting a stray cat chasing a rodent up ahead. Before it slipped between a wall crack and to safety, the cat caught it, trapping it in a paw.

A tremor of unease dashed down Sadie's spine at the sight, a sense of foreboding settling over her as she kept walking, one street after another, her gaze darting about. Hunching her shoulders, she shoved her fists into the front pockets of her trousers and rounded her arms in on her chest. A precaution, a defensive action.

Call it what one may, Sadie only knew every instinct in her body suddenly hollered with the warning to *hide* the moment she rounded the next street corner. Hide her breasts, hide her hips, hide her title—hide *everything*. Like the bells that rang out a fire warning, alarm sounded inside her mind and reverberated throughout her body. In an instant, she knew she was unsafe.

A woman knew such things.

"Who's there?" she called out in a masculine, gruff voice, hoping to fool whoever currently watched her. A bloke not worth trying on. Carenza's harrowing experience with the Revivalists shot to the front of her mind, and Sadie's whole body tensed tight with fear. "I'm a bloody imbecile, stomping off in a huff over a kiss and forgetting my vigilance." The whispered scolding helped, infused her spine with some fire, snapped it straight. "I'll not die tonight out of stupidity." Not tonight or tomorrow or the next day.

Fenchurch Street appeared ahead, and Sadie hurried toward it, thinking the larger street would provide safety. Though she had not been paying much attention, she knew she couldn't be the only person walking around London just now. People needed to return home from their workplaces. That meant people riding horses and walking and taking carriages.

Why, then, did she see no one?

"Strange," Sadie murmured, and burrowed into her worn workman's jacket. Loose cut for ease of movement, it welcomed her into its generous folds as she cast her gaze about nervously. "Where is everyone?"

No longer able to see the setting sun beyond the tall buildings, she stopped briefly to roll up the bottoms of her trousers on the off chance that she might need to run. Fast. The last thing she wanted was to trip on the leg of her pants because they were too long. Escape required immediacy.

Less than three breaths and she was done, back to her fast clip along the usually busy London street. "I don't like this one bit," she muttered, her preoccupation with a certain earl's kiss forgotten with her nerves so quickly unraveling. Ratcheting her cap down on her head, Sadie scanned the darkening streets around her and refused to panic when she noted the empty stores and quiet footpaths. Even the birds seemed to have ceased chattering. "Bloody excellent." This was not good. Truly a bad omen.

Sadie recalled the way West had emptied the Masked Meadowlark in anticipation of a Revivalist attack with a sinking feeling.

Something foul was afoot. And she was caught out in the middle of it, completely alone.

Thankful for the self-defense she had learned, Sadie prepared for a confrontation, knowing that running from a tormentor was generally a futile effort. Unless it was her cousin or the Revivalists. Then she ran. As fast and as far as possible. "All I want is to go home and undo all the blasted bindings around my chest, throw myself on my mattress, perhaps sleep a few precious hours. Is that too much to ask?" She'd discovered that talking to herself often calmed her fears, helped her through a difficult situation.

And she suspected that this would soon be a *very* difficult situation.

"How is London so deserted?" Had a declaration from King William sent everyone scurrying to the countryside or Bath or Yorkshire, or wherever one went when one fled London? Good God, had a plague been unleashed upon its residents?

Laughter, low and menacing, caught her ear from somewhere off in the distance to her right.

Oh God, oh no. Please no. It can't be.

Oh, shite.

Dread pooled in her gut. Sadie knew that laugh, had heard it before. Directly before she had lost consciousness. And right after she had watched West take a knife to his middle.

The Revivalists were on the hunt.

And she was in their path.

Instead of calling out, Sadie shrank and went silent as a mouse, prayed for this to be a nightmare. "I'm asleep and having a bad dream." Yes, that must be it. "I am in my bed in my flat sleeping soundly." Perhaps if she wished it enough, it could be so.

Squeezing her eyes tightly shut for the length of time it took to pray for safety and the gift of speedy feet to outrun a foe, Sadie edged away from the street lamp nearby and crept toward the shadows. Thankfully, her clothing consisted entirely of shades of gray and brown, so she melted into the darkness and disappeared.

Claw their eyes and kick their bollocks in. Smash their instep. Poke. Bite. Go on the attack.

Survive.

Holding her breath to better hear the tiniest sound, Sadie listened for the Revivalists' location, knowing they would not remain silent long. Every news sheet reported on their shocking vocals as they rampaged and pillaged and harmed.

"I will live," she whispered, reiterating it over and over like a prayer and a promise. Whatever it took, she would make it home tonight alive. She had not survived poisoning by her cousin to meet her end at the hands of the most horrendous group of beings to exist on English soil in the last one hundred years. Not since their idols—the last murderous group of aristocrats, the

Mohocks—had terrorized London Town. Oh no, Sadie Wind-crisp, Duchess of Seawell, would carry on to see her duchy returned to her.

Until then, Cousin Archibald held it in her stead, unable to spend a penny of it while awaiting her return. Her father had ensured the bulk of it remained in holding, untouched, until she married. He had allowed a monthly allowance to provide for maintenance of the vast Seawell estate, but even that went directly to the stewards placed throughout the duchy by her father. Each one vetted and trusted. Nothing—and she meant *nothing*—went to her cousin aside from a small monthly stipend for any tribulations suffered as a result of Sadie becoming his ward. A pittance, truly. Not enough to live on, and certainly not enough to elevate her distant cousin's standing amongst Society. No, her father had been a clever, sly gentleman of great wit and heart and insight—and he had seen wisdom in limiting Cousin Archibald's reach to his own arms. Nothing beyond.

While wise, it turned deadly in the wrong hands. In those hands, the only option was death. *Her* death.

Laughter drifted toward her once more, this time carrying a note of impatience as it echoed off the brick buildings lining the streets. The Revivalists wanted quarry, wanted prey. Sadie knew what happened when they found it. A smashing window and raised voices verified their rising discontent.

"No," she breathed, and dashed down the footpath straight ahead, careful to keep her steps light and quiet as she tried to put as much distance between her and the madmen as she could. They had come that night weeks ago for Carenza, and though it had not been a full Revivalist attack, it scared Sadie beyond anything she'd endured before. West had spilled so much blood. It was a blasted miracle he had survived.

"Ahoy there—where do you think you're going?"

Sadie's lungs froze. She couldn't breathe. Couldn't move.

Directly ahead, a man in all black materialized from a small side alleyway and stepped into her path, a club in his hand.

"Leaving so soon?" The masked man shook his head. "The party hasn't even started."

Terror gripped Sadie as she watched another man melt from the darkness and take form before her, joining the first. "Don't rush off. We want to play with you. Don't we, boys?"

"No!" Sadie gasped, recognizing the new man's shape and the way he moved, the sound of his voice. "No!" she shouted again, beginning to shuffle backward and away as quickly as she could. It couldn't be.

He was awful, but a *Revivalist*? How could that be?

Panic rose in her, and she gagged, nearly vomited from the shock of it.

The poisoning attempt suddenly made a lot more sense.

"Oh, I see you. Don't think I don't. Your image is burned in my mind." Archibald chuckled gleefully. "Your face, your height, the way you move. You'll never be able to escape me now." He raised his hand. "Get him, boys." The snarl tore through her cousin, and suddenly Sadie saw a man evil enough to poison her, saw it in his eyes, the curl of his lip into a smile that turned her blood cold.

Run!

Sadie spun around and sprinted down the footpath away from the monsters materializing from the alley to chase after her.

"You're dead, little chap!" her cousin shouted, rage and sick glee entering his voice. "Hear me? *Dead!*"

Her furiously pounding heart was very much alive as Sadie dashed down the first street off Fenchurch she came to, briefly out of sight of the murderers. The building she passed on her right caught her eye with its fanciful architecture and embellishments.

"Let's see if you can keep up with this," Sadie said, and grunted with the effort of launching herself off the ground to grab a jutting bit of windowsill plasterwork far above her head. Grasping it, she quickly swung her legs up and maneuvered to a standing position flush against the building wall, high and out of sight of the Revivalists as they appeared below. "Deal porter skills," she panted, coaxing herself along the ledge. "Well done, Crisp." With fear pushing her on, Sadie shimmied up the building's front, climbing swiftly and precisely over the brick-and-mortar façade until she reached the top.

"Where are you?" her cousin screamed from down below. Crashing windows and shattering glass followed, along with violent swearing and promises of retribution. "I'll find you! I will find you and gut you slow, little chap!" More crashing. "You'll rue the day you crossed the Revivalists!"

Crossed? She'd never bloody been on their side! Christ, her cousin was dicked in the head.

Slowly easing from the edge of the building's flat roof to stand solidly in the middle of it, Sadie released a huge, relieved rush of air that quickly turned into an overwhelmed sob. "This is so, so bad," she whispered, freezing again as she listened to the Revivalists vandalize the street below, calling out for her—well, Thomas Baker.

What was she going to do?

Her cousin wanted her dead. And now he wanted her deal porter persona dead too. The real Sadie and the fake Sadie. Both were now targets.

Her Cousin Archibald, the Revivalist. In a blink her situation had gone from bad to far, far worse. As in, *the* worst.

"How do I proceed from here?" Sadie slowly picked her way across the roof, trembling all the while. Her cousin had taken her life as a duchess from her, and now he'd ruined this one too. What other options could she possibly have? Where else could she go? Perhaps she needed to leave London entirely. Flee to Yorkshire.

Come work for me in my office.

Suddenly the Earl of Castlebury was blocking her vision, his pale blue gaze intense and earnest on hers as he offered her a position in his warehouse doing administrative work. Safe, quiet office tasks, tucked away from public view and prying eyes.

Back straightening with renewed hope, she chose a third option. She, Sadie Crisp, would take Castlebury's offer to be his assistant. Hide somewhere new. *Be* someone new. Not a duchess or a dockworker, but something else entirely.

It might actually work.

But first she needed new hair.

CHAPTER TEN

NOTHING ROBBED CRAWFORD of his goodwill faster than a beautiful day wasted on fruitless, needless endeavors.

"Remember, you agreed to this."

Especially when it was entirely his fault. "Only because you wouldn't stop it with your blasted list," he said around a forced, stiff smile. "My agreement was coerced."

"Stop swearing," Lady Castlebury hissed at him. "I do not tolerate it polluting my ears."

Of course she bloody didn't. "Apologies, Mother." Crawford released a long, drawn-out sigh and prayed for someone to stab him in the eye to relieve him of this misery. The stabbing appealed infinitely more than an afternoon spent deflecting his mother's indelicate attempts at matchmaking and lectures on the necessity of a pristine vocabulary. And if that made him a peevish and unappreciative son, at this juncture, he rather didn't care. "Please excuse me."

Touching his mother's elbow briefly to signal his departure, he had nearly made his escape when a booming voice called out from directly behind him, "Lady Castlebury, how wonderful that you could make it! And who, pray tell, is this handsome young buck standing next to you?"

Bollocks and shite and damn.

"Lord Oliver! Oh, what a delicious event you've arranged to entertain us all with today! The stage design is especially inspired,

I daresay. I simply cannot wait to hear your daughter play her cello!" His mother clapped in emphasis of her enthusiasm for the upcoming musicale. "Neither can my son. Isn't that right, dear?"

Stab him, stab him now. "That's… correct," he begrudgingly offered, though it was decidedly *incorrect.*

His mother laughed, a lilting, tinkling sound that was entirely practiced and artificial. "Silly me!" she said as she sank her fingernails into his arm and anchored him close. Crawford barely resisted the urge to swear, ear pollution and all. "Allow me to make proper introductions. Lord Oliver, may I introduce you to my son, Crawford, Earl of Castlebury?"

Knowing well his duty, he bowed and replied, "It's an honor to meet you, Lord Oliver."

"Please, call me Frederick. Let us not stand on formality." The tall, white-haired marquess smiled amiably at him, and Crawford wanted to do nothing more than escape. That friendly smile came with a catch. And a leg shackle.

No thanks. Not for him. No matter how well she played the cello.

Not even if she played *his* "cello" well.

"Frederick," his mother said with a wide smile. "And where is the star of the afternoon?"

"Ah." Lord Oliver preened under her word choice and looked about the expansive gardens of his home, so rigidly trimmed and tamed, and through the throng of Society milling about the great lawn shorn to a tight crop. "I confess that I do not see Charlotte at this moment." He shrugged his shoulders underneath his finely cut linen jacket and took a sip from his flute of champagne. "Perhaps she is inside warming up her instrument."

I'd like to warm up Sadie's instrument.

Just like that, she was there in the front of his mind, stripped gloriously bare and spread wide for him. Begging him to touch her with her mysterious selkie eyes.

Damnation, what was the matter with him? Vulgarity of language was one thing, something he was perfectly used to. But this luridness of *mind* was entirely new. The worst of it was that it came out of nowhere, unbidden. As if he had no control over his own thoughts. Not since the moment he'd laid eyes on Sadie and felt that strange click inside his mind, that loosening of a lock. That sensation of a key sliding into its rightful place.

It was deuced awful.

"There she is. Charlotte, oh, Charlotte dear!" The marquess waved over the crowd, motioning his daughter to them.

Crawford stifled a groan, catching a glimpse of a tall, slender chit in a blue frock with ruddy cheeks and bright eyes and big teeth. "Let us not disturb her when she is preparing," he said quickly. "I should hate to cause any interruption." Mostly he hated the notion of his mother picking out his bride for him from a list written on a sheet of bloody parchment paper. "In fact," he said, a little desperately, "I shall go sit and eagerly await her performance."

Who said avoidance wasn't a noble choice?

For Crawford, it remained far nobler for him to wait alone in front of the stage than to stand there further while his mother and Lord Oliver snickered together over their perceived cleverness. The two of them were the clumsiest pair of matchmakers he'd ever had the misfortune to witness. Painful, really.

"But shouldn't you rather meet Lady Charlotte before the musicale begins?" Lady Castlebury asked in a pointed tone, her eyes promising retribution should he disobey her suggestion that wasn't really a suggestion.

I would rather throw myself into a pit of venomous snakes.

"Of course, Mother." Inclining his head, he offered her a strained smile. "After you."

Nodding and smiling and playing the part, Crawford made his way across the lawn in the wake of his mother and Lord Oliver. Not in the least bit happy with the current situation, but knowing that he had no legitimate reason to complain—beyond his rather ardent desire to remain unmarried at this particular point in time—he strolled in a leisurely manner with his hands tucked behind his back.

Mostly it was to keep him from ripping that blasted list from his mother's grip and burning it.

"Tell me, have you much affection for the cello?" Lord Oliver inquired as they strolled along the brutally shorn lawn.

"Oh my goodness, yes!" declared Lady Castlebury.

Crawford restrained from snorting in disbelief. His mother had never even mentioned the instrument by name before last week. He wasn't certain before then she had known they existed as a unique class of strings.

When they reached the other side of the lawn, Lord Oliver called for his daughter. "Charlotte, do come here!"

He couldn't do it. As much as he loved his mother and the rest of his family, Crawford simply couldn't do it. "I'm going to be sick," he muttered, not knowing if he meant that in the literal sense or symbolic, and uncaring either way. Anyone other than him determining choices and decisions in his life made him feel utterly ill inside. Also furious. But first and foremost, sick as a dog who'd eaten too many kitchen scraps.

Do your duty, Crawford.

His father's words burned in his mind—words he had heard so often they'd been a type of mantra in his youth. Exactly as they always did, they stirred resentment and resignation and anger and family honor into a bubbling brew inside him. Equal parts. Wholly upsetting. It gave him indigestion.

"It's delightful to meet you, Lady Charlotte," he said dutifully, regardless of his burgeoning gastric discomfort. "I'm told you've quite the talent with a cello." Witness him being a proper earl. He even offered the young lady a mostly genuine smile. For upon close inspection, she looked about as pleased with this introduction as he felt. Perhaps his concerns had been for naught. Good God, wouldn't that be a relief? A much-appreciated reprieve.

"Thank you, Lord Castlebury." The marquess's daughter glanced at him through her lashes—and he caught the flash of fire, defiance, and heartache. Yes, nothing to fear there. "I've practiced it since I was a child. If I am not proficient by now, I fear I shall never be."

She belonged to another—in heart if not by law. One marriageable miss struck off his mother's deplorable list.

"Do you know, now that I think upon it, who else possessed a fondness for playing the cello?" Lord Oliver mused, his gaze going unfocused with distant memory. "The late Duchess of Seawell." He made a quick sign of respect to the deceased and continued, "I do believe she passed that talent on to her daughter, Lady Sadie, who used to play alongside her when they hosted their annual musicale at their exquisite townhome on Park Lane. I confess I quite believed Lady Sadie to be a brilliant musician. It is such a shame what happened to the duke and duchess last year."

Even Crawford had heard the harrowing story of how they had died in an inn fire while traveling to Edinburgh.

"Absolutely heartbreaking," his mother agreed, and meant it. Crawford knew she had been on friendly terms with the duchess. "Do you know," she began in a thoughtful tone, "I don't believe I have seen Lady Sadie in recent months. Not since shortly after the passing of the duke and duchess. Have you?"

"I say, I have not!" Lord Oliver replied with surprised realization. "Ah, I'll wager she's still mourning their passing."

"After a year?" Lady Charlotte asked. "That seems a rather long time to stay in mourning."

The marquess shrugged his narrow shoulders, the movement barely perceptible beneath his navy tailcoat. "We all grieve in our own way and time, my dear."

Crawford had to agree with Lady Charlotte. It did seem a tad odd. "Perhaps a friendly visit to her address, then? That should clear the air quite sufficiently, I'd say."

"Or perhaps you could ask her guardian?" Lady Charlotte was proving to be a rather practical sort. It was greatly appreciated. "I believe he's her distant cousin or some such person. He took over residence of the Park Lane townhouse."

"How do you possess all this information?" the marquess asked.

"Lady Sadie and I were playmates and friends on occasion. I paid attention when her parents passed to learn what would become of her."

"Rather kind of you, dearest," approved Lord Oliver. "Should we make our way to our seats? I confess I'm eager to hear your latest pick from Beethoven's repertoire."

"Yes, I hope you are pleased, Father. Signore Fallotini and I have worked very hard together to perfect today's pieces." The way Lady Charlotte's eyes lit up with emotion when she mentioned her cello instructor's name told Crawford *exactly* where her heart resided, and with whom.

While *he* wished for no attachments, Lady Charlotte clearly was quite thoroughly attached to Signore Fallotini. Crawford supposed that the only thing worse than a forced marriage was a life lived without the one loved with a full heart.

Compassion for his current companion filled him. They might not be destined for marriage, but he did rather like her. That their parents had coordinated to bring them together with the expectation they would match up without fuss provided a common ground for his appreciation.

"Lady Charlotte?" He offered his elbow, knowing his mother would assign a thousand different meanings to his action. "Would you do me the honor of accompanying me to the audience seats? I admit that I am also eager to hear your performance of Beethoven's cello music. He was quite the radical musician. I spent an evening with him in Vienna once, before he fell ill. It was during my Grand Tour."

"Are you quite serious, my lord?" Lady Charlotte eyed him skeptically, a discerning trait he admired.

Crawford nodded as she took his offered elbow, her hands sliding over the refined linen of his jacket sleeve. "I am being utterly sincere in this account. Truly. He got foxed as anything and played the most extraordinary musical piece anyone there that evening had ever heard—a movement he created right there without any forethought. Unfortunately, he had no recollection of the piece the next day. Too many spirits had wiped it clean from his memory."

"Are you jesting, my lord? You must be jesting." Lady Charlotte pursed her lips and considered him. "I think you're jesting."

Crawford laughed, surprised to discover himself not completely hating the day's outing or foisted-upon companion after all.

His mother was going to be impossible after this.

CHAPTER ELEVEN

Q UIET. BLESSED, GLORIOUS quiet.
Finally.

Tucked into her tiny bit of home atop the haberdashery, Sadie sighed into the cushions of her one bit of luxury: a faded gold chaise with threadbare patches of upholstery that had been stored there years ago by Herr Olsen. Frau Olsen had forgotten all about it until Sadie appeared to rent the attic space and they both discovered its presence. With nothing more than a small travel bag in her possession, she had been relieved and grateful to be given a place to sit and rest. Though the chaise was ugly, it was comfortable—proven thoroughly by all the nights she had spent sleeping on it before acquiring enough funds to purchase a mattress.

So perhaps that was two bits of luxury? After five months of her curling into a ball to fit the limited area of the chaise, the mattress stretched wide and flat across the ancient plank floorboards had felt decadent. Sadie would never again take for granted the wonderful freedom a bed provided. When she once again slept in her own bed at Park House—the one with the thick wooden bedposts carved with intricate patterns of vines and flowers that climbed upward to the smoothly rounded tops—she would give thanks. As a child she would trace the carvings' paths with her fingers in the dark when sleep eluded her. She knew every leaf curl, every slender stem lovingly rendered into the glossy oak.

Emotion snagged in Sadie's chest and caught her off guard.

Oh, she missed it! Missed terribly that bit of comfort and history—of belonging to something and somewhere larger and longer lasting than herself. She ached for that simple, old familiarity. For the history that went hand in hand with such things.

Her childhood in a bedpost.

"If he's sleeping in my bed, I promise he'll regret it." Someday. Not today or tomorrow—or likely even next month. But someday Cousin Archibald would get his comeuppance.

Life would come back around on him.

"Knock, knock! Frau Baker, are you in there?"

Sadie groaned. *"Nooo."* There went her blessed peace and quiet. Dropping her head down against the chaise back, she looked up to the sloped roof and inhaled a fortifying breath. "Good evening, Frau Olsen!" she called back, remembering her manners. "Can I help you?"

"No," replied the widow as she opened the narrow plank door with its creaky hinges and slipped inside. Even late in the evening, she appeared as pressed and neat as when the day began. An admirable trait that Sadie could not even hope to possess. So she didn't even try. "Perhaps I can assist *you*, however."

Oh, did she happen to have the ability to rid London of her cousin, then?

No? *Drat.* "Perhaps you can," Sadie replied agreeably, though she doubted it.

"A missive arrived for you." Frau Olsen handed her a sealed and folded bit of parchment. "I received it while you were clanging about with your dinner pots."

Her own attempt at stew. The result… not good.

"Thank you for bringing this to me," Sadie said as she rose from the chaise in her modest floral printed dressing gown, her heavy hair sliding over her shoulder to pour loose down her back. "I can't imagine who it is from."

"Handsome, intriguing fellow delivered it," Frau Olsen said with a smile and blush.

If Sadie wasn't wrong, a hint of girlish delight had entered Frau Olsen's tone at the mention of the deliveryman. Certainly, it had entered her gaze.

Well, goodness.

Was *Frau* perhaps ready to meet another *Herr*?

Prying the seal of the letter loose, Sadie noted the signature pressed into the wax, and raised a brow curiously. Damon was sending her a missive. Why?

"I'll just be a moment," she mumbled distractedly to Frau Olsen, already scanning the letter.

Your name is all over the back-alley gossip. Seems your cousin is asking around Covent Garden for you, and down at the docks for a bloke described like you, but in trousers and a cap.

Careful. I don't like how close he's sniffing.

Demon

Sadie smirked over the *ton*'s moniker for Damon, though they now had to address him as Viscount Amslee instead. Must hurt them, swallowing that one, looking him in the eye and knowing that he knew—that he'd been *paid* to know. And that now he held their money *and* their secrets and walked amongst them as a peer. Oh, how that must chafe.

It helped knowing she was not the only black sheep of the *ton*.

Well, perhaps "black sheep" misstated it a bit. Her childhood rearing had been rather warm and wonderful, and Society had welcomed her readily as the only child of a duke. Suitors had thrown themselves in her path. When no one gained her affections her debut Season, Father had merely chuckled and called them all fools, wished her a better go-around next time.

The black sheep bit came from living on the outside, knowing that she should belong, but didn't. Maybe never would again. For the foreseeable future she remained in hiding. *If* she could stay hidden. Her cousin's snooping could bode very ill for her. Very ill indeed.

"Frau Olsen," she began as she refolded the letter and placed it in a pocket of her dressing gown, "I've been thinking of changing my hair. It's so heavy, you see. Gives me headaches." Sadie grimaced and rubbed a temple with her finger for emphasis. "Would you happen to be handy with a pair of kitchen shears?"

The sturdy-bodied woman pursed her lips and looked Sadie over with a critical eye. "As a matter of fact…" she replied with a slight smile, her eyes brightening with interest. "I imagine you have a particular style in mind, *ja?*"

"As one would have it, I do." Sadie grinned back.

"Something daring?" Frau Olsen quirked a brow.

"Absolutely bold," Sadie replied with a laugh of delight.

"And Herr Baker?"

"Won't even recognize me." That was exactly the point. To be unrecognizable.

"I'll retrieve my shears and return momentarily."

Sadie bit her lip to contain her nerves and the budding excitement such a physical change could bring about. Then she thought about her cousin and his part in the Revivalists and how it should be simple to go to Bow Street, but it wasn't. Archibald was her guardian. Even if she accused him, even if Captain Castlebury believed her, by all English rule, her cousin owned her. If she came out of hiding, she would simply be deposited right back into Cousin Archibald's evil hands. And her concerns would be brushed aside, disregarded as a momentary lapse of sense, given her delicate womanly disposition. On the off chance they listened and chose to investigate, she would *still* be returned to her cousin.

"I have kitchen shears!"

Sadie swallowed the emotion rising in her throat and forced a smile. "Let's begin, then."

"How daring?" Frau Olsen asked, her shrewd eyes assessing Sadie's countenance.

She took a deep breath, felt the niggles in her belly. Knew

what she had to do regardless.

"Make it as daring as it gets."

Lord Castlebury was late. Unsurprising, given the vast wealth of his earldom. Aristocrats such as him probably didn't even rise before the noon meal. Too exhausted from an evening of debauchery and drink. Though she supposed drink could be counted as a type of debauchery, so perhaps an evening of all-inclusive debauching.

Sadie uncrossed and recrossed her booted ankles underneath the layers of chemise and skirt fabric. "Too much bloody material," she muttered, much preferring the freedom of movement provided by her trousers and tunic. Which was fairly ironic, given her love of beautiful gowns. Admiring their aesthetics was one thing. Wearing them was another entirely. "Blasted half-corsets and whale boning and laces long enough to strangle a person with." Some parts of her personality had performed the most dramatic change of all. Such as her needless swooning over fine lace or elegant satin. These past months of humility and modesty had taught her that while such things were lovely, they were not necessary. A satisfying life, a safe and happy one, did not rely upon luxurious fabrics and a bias cut. It blossomed from within when one chose a life of purpose. Whatever that purpose was—so long as it harmed no one—if a person pursued that path, a well of satisfaction sprang forth from which to quench one's thirst.

This duchess had learned a few life lessons. Changed. Grown. Become emboldened.

Transformed.

Sadie touched a finger to a close-cropped curl and felt it brush her temple. *I wonder what he'll think of it.*

No, she didn't. "Do not," she muttered. Sitting up as straight as she was able while continuing to draw adequate breath, Sadie dropped her fingers from her newly shorn strands and immediately began fidgeting with a tiny loose thread on the sleeve of her light brown day dress. "What have we here?" she inquired with a narrowed eye. "I thought I had performed all repairs on this sleeve." It was her one good dress. The one she wore to appear as a proper young lady to London's citizens.

If they only knew.

"May I help you?"

Sadie jumped, startled by the deeply masculine voice coming from directly above her head. "Oh!" she cried softly, instantly recognizing it. Immediately feeling foolish and strangely invigorated at the same time, Sadie bit her bottom lip as she prepared to look up into the startlingly handsome face of Lord Castlebury.

"This is a private office suite. Perhaps you are lost, miss?" A hint of impatience peppered his tone. "I would be glad to assist you to the building's entrance."

Polished, comfortably worn, tall boots of a rich brown leather appeared in her vision as Sadie took a steadying moment. Why did the earl seem to have such a breathless, unsettling effect on her? It plucked her every nerve, knowing she possessed such a response to him.

"I will be glad to assist *you*, my lord." Sadie braced for the impact and raised her gaze.

A four-in-hand slammed into her, pummeled her to the ground.

"My God," Lord Castlebury breathed, echoing her exact thoughts. "Sadie."

She touched her short curls self-consciously but offered him a wavering smile. "In the flesh."

Lightning heated his blue gaze. "I-I did not recognize you."

"It's the dress, isn't it?" she jested, covering up her response to him with a joke as she shot from the chair, unable to bear his towering form over her and the closeness. Too many nerves. "It always confuses people."

"Your hair," he murmured, his gaze fixed on the top of her head. "Has it always been this short?"

"A recent change," she replied, touching the freshly cut ends again. No longer heavy as a curtain, her strands sprang about her head with silken lightness. The sensation rather pleased her. As did the way he continued to look at her. It sent heat swirling through her belly.

"I like it."

The way he said the words, so straightforward and honest, simple, turned her knees to jelly. "Th-thank you," she replied, unable to look away from his crystalline blue gaze. "I, um, needed a change."

"You have most definitely changed."

The way the earl said it, all low and laced with innuendo, had Sadie's breath hitching in her chest. Sucking in a great gasp of air, she did not notice until it was too late that the motion shoved her breasts up and out toward Lord Castlebury like a tray of delicacies presented for his sampling. Of course his gaze dropped to the rounded bodice of her dress and the swell of her bosom just barely visible.

Her skin reacted as if he had traced his fingers along the delicate curve. Goose pimples rose along her arms, and a thrill of feminine excitement darted down her spine. "Only on the outside," she finally managed to say.

"Selkie," Lord Castlebury whispered, stepping closer to her, his big, hard body radiating an irresistible heat.

"I, uh," Sadie sputtered, her mind overwhelmed with the sight and smell and closeness of the sexiest male she had ever seen. Oh, how she wished she could squeeze her eyes shut and dismiss him, regain her control! But she couldn't even blink. All she could do was stare at his rich, auburn-colored hair as his head seemed to lower closer to hers. Her fingers—those traitorous digits—trembled with the desire to feel those autumn-hued strands gliding between them. She swallowed. "I'm here to accept your offer for the office assistant position."

"Is that so?" Castlebury raised a russet brow, his gaze taking on a wicked glint as it returned to hers.

Sadie nodded emphatically, her heart thumping in her chest. Everything about the earl unnerved her. Not wholly and entirely in a bad way. And *that* unnerved her even more. "Yes, it is so."

"It's rather early in the morning, don't you think?"

He really needed to stop looking at her that way! "No, my lord, I think it is a perfectly reasonable hour to arrive."

"It's dock hours."

What did that matter? "And?"

His eyes, they simply mesmerized.

"This is an office."

"And?" She truly did not understand the issue. "It is an office at the docks." Why, his eyes held tiny specks of cobalt in them. *Sigh.* Sadie leaned a tiny smidge closer.

"Office hours differ than dock hours."

"Oh." Blast, but he smelled good. Sadie inched closer still, sniffed delicately. "They do?" She was a duchess by birth and deal porter by necessity. How was she to know such things?

"Mm-hmm," he murmured, his nose and mouth remarkably close to her ear now. "They do." His deep, cultured voice so near sent delicious chills racing along her skin. "You've two hours yet before you are due to arrive."

"Oh," she repeated, unable to think of anything wittier than that with his breath trailing hot and scintillating down her neck. "Then we're agreed?" she inquired, her breath thready. "I've the position?"

"Do you want this position under me?" Castlebury murmured against her ear, his tone rough with suggestion. She went boneless against the hallway wall. Damn, but she liked this coarser side of him. Evidence of too much time on the docks. The duchess who'd arrived that first day would have disapproved.

But this duchess *very* much approved. "I do," she whispered, and gasped when his teeth gently scraped the curve of her ear. Liquid heat bloomed between her thighs.

"Should we seal the agreement with a kiss?"

The words echoed in her mind, made her reckless. "Yes," she agreed on a moan. But then an undeniable urge swept her up and along with it, and Sadie had no time to do anything more than react. "Except," she countered, bringing her hands up to frame his face and hold him still while she looked him square in the eye, "this time, *I'm* kissing *you.*"

Lord Castlebury's eyes widened a fraction in surprise before her lips claimed his.

Kiss him, she did.

CHAPTER TWELVE

H E BLAMED THE hair.

Yesterday, Crawford had taken one look at that glossy crop of brunette curls and the way it had made her emerald eyes appear so round and intoxicating—and he'd fallen, so pathetically deep into lust and infatuation that seeing through the fog it caused had been impossible. All he'd been able to do was kiss Sadie in a way that was neither wholesome nor decent. It had been dirty as hell.

Dueling tongues and hot lips and impatient, stroking hands up surprisingly shapely legs with the smoothest, softest skin on her inner thigh so near that hidden palace. Her place of worship. Christ, how he wanted to worship her there.

Groaning, Crawford scrubbed a hand over his face and slowly rotated around in his office chair. "Today, I will behave," he promised. Yesterday he had not, and he had spent the entirety of the rest of the day in profound discombobulation, his body in utter chaos. His mind had been no better. Rather unfortunate, considering that once he had returned from the docks to Tipton House, his mother had immediately dragged him off to the opera at Rhodes Theatre, where she had increased her matchmaking efforts. Eligible miss after miss had been paraded in front of him like potential broodmares for the picking.

Have you had the pleasure of an introduction to…?

I would like you to meet Miss…

Such a delightful dear! Crawford, have you yet met…?

Goodness, such a talent! You must meet my son, Lord Castlebury…

It was enough to make him sick. And this morning, well, he nearly looked it, as if he had spent the night with his insides heaving outside and tangling into knots. Between an onslaught of unwanted women, and unsated desire for one extremely *wanted* woman, he hadn't slept well. It had been a lot of tossing and turning and muttering and staring at the ceiling.

As earl he should marry one of the many ridiculous women his mother herded in his direction. He knew that. The simplest, most traditional path. The right one. The *only* one, really.

But he didn't want those women. He wanted *one* woman. One he knew not at all yet couldn't get out of his head. Even if he *did* know her well, she did not suit, did not fit the requirements set forth for the wife of an earl. Because she was a commoner. Because she had no pedigree.

"Shite rules, if you ask me." Crawford rotated the rest of the way around in his chair and huffed out a breath, glancing at the darkness still lingering through the window and out over London Docks beyond. Dawn would soon approach, but for now the quiet blanket of night still covered the land. "Damon was just Damon when Carenza chose him." Not that he was considering choosing Sadie Crisp. Definitely not. Deuce it, he didn't even know anything about her!

And it bloody well bothered the hell out of him. Who was she? Where did she come from? Why was she hiding?

Did she belong to somebody?

The thought sent a wave of jealousy coursing through him.

"What the devil?" Crawford jerked up in his seat and slammed his boot heels flat on the floor. Him? Jealous? Absurd! He did not get jealous.

More precisely, there had never been a woman worthy of becoming jealous over.

She is, his mind whispered.

"Oh, shut up," Crawford snapped at his conscience. "No one

bloody asked you."

Even if she was worth it, he still couldn't choose her. Even if he wanted to. No matter that his body raged with desire for her. *I'm randy as an adolescent boy in a room full of bared breasts.* It made no difference. Someday he would marry, and it would not be to common-born Sadie Crisp. Even if she did capture his imagination. And turn his cock to stone.

Ah, hell. He needed to stop talking to himself now. It was only going from bad to worse.

"The woman of your dreams directly in front of you, and she is wholly ineligible. Blame your bloody aristocratic station for the inequality in pairing—not her lack of one. It's your kind that traps and hobbles and hinders with all their absurd rules." Crawford snatched a colorful West Indian paperweight from the oversized desk in front of him. "Look at this. It's beautiful. From humble origins, but look how it shines." Should he blame it for being made of a modest material and not porcelain?

No, he should not. It held beauty in its own right. Deserving of admiration and appreciation. Respect.

For several minutes Crawford sat in silence, taking in the stillness of predawn, lost in his thoughts. Unable to rest after his mother's parade of eligible ladies, he had found himself returning to Warehouse No. 3 and his father's lumpy sofa. Like Winslow Castlebury, he had finally found rest there for a few precious hours, the sound of water lapping against the quay outside the open window lulling him to sleep.

A fever-hot dream of Sadie had awakened him. Exactly in time, too. He really hadn't fancied a soiled pair of trousers to contend with.

But now… now he ached for her.

He reached down and rubbed his erection through his trousers. Stifled a groan.

"Good morning, Lord Castlebury. I am aware that it's quite early—do not lecture me."

Crawford yanked his hand from his cock and jumped, slamming a knee into the bottom of the desk. Pain exploded at the contact, and he swore. "Miss Crisp," he managed around a hiss of discomfort. Self-consciousness flooded him and burned high in his cheeks. Christ, how much had she seen? "I, ahem, did not hear your approach."

"That's because you weren't paying attention."

No mention of his hand placement or what he had been about to do. *Excellent. Capital, really.* "Apologies. I hadn't the expectation of such an early visitor."

"Not a visitor," she said primly, sweeping into the room with a large satchel in hand. "I've come to work." She waved a gloved hand around, looking far too tempting for his addled brain to cope with. "It's clear that this office is in need of attendance and organization. I'm well aware that there has been no one of note tending to the books since Dobbs's unfortunate accident. I'm here to begin setting those to rights and to get the ordering system flowing smoothly again."

Far too much intelligence coming at him all at once. His brain still currently resided within his bollocks.

"I…" he started, and stopped to swallow against a suddenly parched throat. "I, ahem, am thankful for your assistance."

"Well"—Sadie unceremoniously dropped her satchel down— "let's get to it, shall we? The day is already wasting."

No. Yes. Anything she wanted. Christ, he couldn't think in her presence. But oh, how he wanted to stare. At her. *Everywhere.*

"Yes, let's do," he murmured, soaking in the sight of her from his position behind the desk. "Where should we start?"

And off she went. They spent the day poring over records and transactions and ledgers—and with every sign of her wit and intelligence and organizational skills, Crawford fell harder, wanted deeper. With every brush of her hand against his, with every heated glance and flirtatious smile, their desire flared. By the end of the day, as sunset drew to a close outside the office windows of Castle Shipping, he knew he had to have her.

What surprised him was that she felt that way too.

And she beat him to it. "Now, let's turn our attention to other matters," she suggested.

"Such as?" he asked, his body tensing in anticipation.

"Us."

"Us?" he echoed, his cock stirring excitedly.

"I think it's time." She tipped her head to the side, her emerald eyes glittering with meaning. "Don't you?"

He did. Christ yes, he did.

"Anyplace, anytime," he answered.

She looked at him, smiling. "Here and now."

CHAPTER THIRTEEN

"**I** LIKE YOUR office space, Crawford, and I want you. I do not want to wait another moment. Seems rather pointless to in light of that fact, don't you agree?"

Crawford stared hard at Sadie, his chest suddenly tight and constricting. He watched in fascination as she took off her ankle boots and placed them neatly to the side of her chair. Desire shot through him as he raked his eyes up her stocking-covered feet to her arms that were raised to her hair. Realizing that she was removing the pins from the cap that hid her lustrous hair finally spurred Crawford into motion.

"Let me do that," he offered as he strode over to her. Coming to a stop behind her, Crawford sank to his knees on the Persian rug and gently pushed Sadie's hands aside. "I've wanted nothing more than to sink my hands into it since you cut it. You did it on purpose just to further tempt me, didn't you, Selkie?"

She smiled over her shoulder at Crawford, her heart flooded with emotions. Anticipation filled her, lending a sweet feeling of giddiness to her lustful body.

Crawford leaned toward Sadie and slid his hand up the front of her throat, the warmth of his large palm seeping into her. Cupping her throat and the bottom of her jaw, Crawford tilted her head back further. With his eyes on hers, he began to one-handedly remove the pins from her bonnet. Quickly, Sadie's hat tumbled from her head and fell to the carpet of soft wool below.

She could see the pulse beating heavily in his neck, the tenseness of his jaw.

Dragging his gaze from her hair, Crawford glanced at her and whispered, "I have wanted to do this since the first time I saw you."

Sadie's lips parted softly as she gazed up at Crawford, and her breath began to come in short spurts, her breathing quick and shallow. Feminine wariness crept into her eyes, making his lips curve wolfishly as Crawford wound his free hand in her thick, short crop of hair and grasped a handful. Gently, he tugged Sadie's head back, holding her prisoner against his chest. Her heart skipped a beat at the purely wicked smile on his face and the scorching heat in his eyes.

On a low laugh, he finally spoke. "It's too late for you to change your mind, selkie mine. There will be no turning back now. You want me, and now I'm going to claim you."

Excited fear skittered along her nerves at the possessive look in Crawford's eyes. Boldly, she replied, her head still held in place, "Do your worst, Crawford Castlebury. Claim me if you can, but know I'm claiming you as well."

She saw the lust that went raging through Crawford's blood at her brazen words. "Christ, I love your fire. You make me crazy with desire and longing. You gift me with one of your smiles and my heart races like a schoolboy's." With a wicked laugh, Crawford stroked his finger up Sadie's jaw, over her chin, to trace the fullness of her lower lip. "You are a brazen wench, Sadie, love. You're claiming me as well, are you?"

Sadie opened her mouth and quickly nipped the pad of Crawford's finger, causing him to jerk and draw in a sharp breath, his eyes flashing hotly. "I believe it goes both ways, does it not?"

"With us it does, love. With us it does."

Lowering his mouth, Crawford captured Sadie's lips in a drugging kiss. The hard hand on her throat slid slowly downward to her chest, coming to rest just above the edge of her bodice.

Like a kitten enjoying a stroke, Sadie arched into Crawford's hand, seeking the heat of his large palm. He traced his fingers along the edge of her dress, slipping ever so slightly inside.

At the same moment as he slid his fingers inside her dress, he slipped his tongue inside her silky mouth. Stroking, his tongue teased and tantalized, making Sadie yearn for more.

Crawford's strong fingers trailed a path over the firm mounds of her breasts and the valley between, gently setting her skin on fire. Sadie's nipples grew taut with arousal; her breasts grew full and tender to his touch. Needing more of his erotic touch, Sadie whimpered into his hot mouth and arched as far into his hand as she could manage.

Laughing softly against her lips, Crawford whispered, "You like the way I touch you, love. You crave more of me."

It was not a question.

Sadie opened her heavy lids, gazed into Crawford's glittering eyes, and nodded, her voice breathless to her ears. "Yes, and it's time I knew how you plan to claim me. Show me."

He released Sadie's silky hair and glided that hand to the buttons on her dress. Releasing them from their place, Crawford slowly, deliberately tugged her dress down, revealing the creamy perfection of her firm breasts. Raspberry-colored nipples jutted out, budded tight with need.

Whispering roughly in her ear, he began inching the skirt of her dress up her thighs, "You are perfection. You make it very hard to go slow and easy when I see such beauty in your body. It is a wonderland I want nothing more than to explore until I know every inch. Every dip, every curve." Running his palm along the inside of her thigh, Crawford nipped her ear and continued. "I'll discover every single sensitive, sweet spot on your body."

She felt his rough hand creeping up her warm thighs and fought the instinctive urge to close her legs tight against intrusion. Crawford's soft chuckle urged her to open fully to him, to spread her legs wide. A quick intake of breath behind her told her he approved of her boldness. Encouraged, Sadie looked up at him and quietly demanded, "Touch me. Touch me where I have been dying for you to touch me."

Crawford fondled her soft mounds, let his hand learn their weight and texture. Sadie released a soft moan when his rough thumb flicked playfully over her pearled nipple. Again, he flicked his finger over her aroused bud, making her bite her lip from the sweet sensation.

Kissing the underside of her ear, Crawford growled against her neck, sending shivers of awareness down Sadie's spine. Her mind was so focused on his mouth against her tender skin and his calloused hand on her breast that she did not feel his other hand releasing the stays of her undergarments.

A rush of pure lust shot straight to her core when Crawford pinched her taut nipple between his thumb and index finger and erotically bit the extremely sensitive skin just beneath her ear. Sadie arched back against him and let loose a throaty groan. "Yes." Reaching her hands back, she grasped Crawford's head and pulled him around for a hot, thorough kiss. The aggressor in that area now, Sadie licked his firm lips and pushed her tongue inside his mouth, stroking his tongue with her own.

Desire roared to life, almost overwhelming Sadie with its intensity.

Sensing the shift in her, Crawford flattened his palm against the warm skin on her lower abdomen and slowly edged downward. Coming in contact with the soft, springy curls, he continued on, his fingers teasing until he came to her hidden slit.

Sadie held her breath in lustful anticipation; her crotch throbbed hot and heavy, begging for something only Crawford could give her. When he cupped her fully, heat poured from her center, making her shift against his hand, searching to ease the ache. "That's it, love. I'm going to make you beg for me in a moment, Sadie, so desperate will you be. Only I will be able to appease your need. Only I. I can already feel your desire for me. You belong to me now, and I'm going to take you over the edge."

Not understanding his words, Sadie grabbed a handful of Crawford's hair and tugged. Needing no further encouragement, he opened Sadie's slick folds with a strong finger and began to explore.

She gasped at the flood of sensation, making Crawford smile against her. "You are so wet for me. So incredibly wet. Do you like it when I do this, love?" He slipped his thumb between her folds and found her clitoris. His heart rolled in his chest at Sadie's unpracticed reaction to him. She jerked against the sudden rush of concentrated sensation, holding on to his hair like it were a lifeline. Dropping her head back against his chest, Sadie moaned deep, the sound full of heady passion.

Crawford circled the tight bud with his thumb, watching Sadie's sweet face intently. It was flushed with arousal, and her lush lips were parted on a silent whimper. Her eyes were shut, long sable lashes casting shadows over her cheekbones.

He was watching her so intently, Crawford noticed when her breathing became more erratic, and her brow pulled down in intense concentration. Sadie began to shift, lifting to meet his stroking fingers. Suddenly, he pushed a long finger deep inside, and she screamed out softly, bucking against his palm, gripping his shoulders tightly for support.

Hunger clawed at Crawford, demanding he take Sadie now. Never before had he witnessed such open passion. It was the most erotic, sensual experience of his life to watch Sadie come unraveled, consumed by desire. Emotions swirled in Crawford as he watched her writhe and moan beneath his questing hands. A dangerous emotion welled up, but he forcefully pushed it aside and concentrated on Sadie.

Wanting her naked, Crawford kept his hand where it was but slowly edged out from behind Sadie. Opening eyes that were unfocused and glazed, she looked at him in confusion. Crushing his mouth to hers, he maneuvered his way out from behind her. Holding her head with his free hand, Crawford lowered Sadie to the ground, kissing her fiercely all the way.

Breaking the kiss, she asked, "Is this it?"

Smiling with great tenderness, he replied, "No, love, this is still the beginning. I want you naked, is all. I need to see all of you, touch all of you."

Sadie gazed up at Crawford's bare chest, at the soft sprinkling of hair there. An urge to see all of that muscular body unhindered by clothing made her say, "I want you naked as well, Crawford. Let me see you unclothed."

He laughed wickedly and yanked at a stocking. "You first."

Quickly they divested themselves of their clothing, and Crawford sat back to admire Sadie. "You are beautiful. Amazing." Strong, curvy legs, wonderfully firm hips, full breasts, and that wonderfully soft belly that drove him mad. The kind of belly that screamed femininity and all things woman.

Crawford raked his hungry gaze over her, while Sadie stared in a mixture of arousal and fascination at his sculpted body. It was nothing like she had imagined in her dreams. He was all hard, disciplined muscle.

Letting her gaze lower to his cock, Sadie gasped. Hard and heavy, it jutted out between his legs, the base of his erection concealed by rich auburn curls. The plump head pushed out toward Sadie in silent warning, sending a thrill of anticipation to the very core of her.

Noticing her reaction to his arousal, Crawford stroked her legs and said, "Don't be afraid, love. I won't hurt you, I promise."

Sadie continued to stare at his hard length, feeling a heavy, hungry ache swell desperately between her thighs as she did. Needy, impatient claws tugged at her, making her look up at him and state, "You misunderstand, Crawford. I am not afraid. Looking at it makes me feel needy and lustful."

Heat flared deep in Crawford's eyes, and he smiled, wickedly and full of promise. "Good, that's good, because you haven't seen anything yet, love."

Crawford slipped a hand back up her thigh to the slick folds and began caressing. Instantly the ache between Sadie's thighs surged to life again, pulsing with renewed vigor. Opening wider for him, she let her head fall back in surrender.

Crawford watched as he glided his hand over Sadie's most private flesh. His heart beat thick and slow in his chest as she gave over to him what no other man had touched. A raw, primitive possessiveness stole over Crawford at the thought. Sadie was his, and a need so strong he couldn't deny it led him to look her in the eye and say, "I'm going to kiss you now, Sadie, the way I've been wanting to so desperately. The way a man kisses a woman he can't get enough of."

She slowly nodded her head and opened her arms to him. "Kiss me, Crawford. Show me how a man kisses a woman he can't get enough of."

He shook his head, the look in his blue eyes wild and dangerous. "No, love, not that type of kissing. Spread your legs wider and you'll soon see what I mean."

Sadie looked on in passionate confusion as Crawford positioned himself between her thighs. Not entirely certain what it was he wished to do, she trusted him regardless and opened her legs.

Caressing the tender flesh of Sadie's inner thighs, Crawford hungrily gazed at her dark curls, his stomach curling tighter and tighter with vicious need. The urge to bury himself in her hot sheath was becoming almost excruciating, but he resisted, sweat pearling on his brow and unshaven upper lip from effort.

Slowly, he lowered his head and began teasing her puckered nipple with the tip of his tongue. Shocked by the sensation, Sadie jerked upward and let out a soft "Oh." Crawford smiled up at her and slowly drew her tight bud into his mouth for a drugging moment. His tongue slowly swirled around and around as his hot mouth created a gentle suction.

Heat glided along Sadie's skin to the center of her stomach as Crawford continued his gentle assault. Soon she found herself writhing beneath him, her hands in his hair holding him tight to her chest. Just when she didn't think the pleasure could become any more intense, he nipped sensually at her nipple and tugged gently, sending shards of sharp pleasure straight to the pool of desire in the pit of her stomach.

Crawford grinned to himself, thrilled at her passionate responses, and trailed wet kisses to her other breast. Lavishing the same attention on that breast, he became aware of the heightening of Sadie's pleasure, her desire.

Soft pants were coming from her now, her head rolled to the side, her hands holding his head to her. Tugging her nipple between his teeth, Crawford watched as Sadie arched her back toward him and let out a low, throaty moan.

No longer able to deny himself, he rained open-mouthed kisses down her stomach and dipped his tongue in and around Sadie's belly button, drawing a sharp intake of breath from her. When he reached the apex of her thighs, desire leapt inside him like a pouncing lion, roaring frighteningly to life. The need to brand her his with his mouth and tongue, then his body, drove him down, where he slipped his tongue between her slit and found her most private pleasure peak.

A loud groan escaped Sadie as she arched her body toward Crawford in silent bid for more. Letting her legs fall to the side, she gasped, "Is this what you meant, Crawford?"

With his fingers gently spreading her, Crawford thrust his tongue inside, growling with his own pleasure. How hot she tasted. How deliciously wet and ready she was for him. He slid his tongue up to her most sensitive bud and suckled gently.

"Yes, love, this is how I've been dreaming of kissing you. You're so hot, Sadie. I want to make you come before I claim you. Let me love you."

She dropped her head back and let him love her, tension coiling tight in her stomach. The incredible pleasure built uncontrollably, and Crawford increased his relentless assault. Forcefully, he stroked his tongue over her woman's bud, urging her further and further toward an unknown end.

Bucking and panting, Sadie tossed her head from side to side, her mind cleared of everything but Crawford's mouth on her, driving her relentlessly toward *something*. Tension began to center and coil heavy in the pit of her stomach.

Afraid of what was happening, she begged, "Crawford,

please."

Urging her on now with mouth and fingers, he soothed her, "That's it, love. Ride it. Don't be afraid. Relax and let it take you over the edge. I want to see you come, Sadie."

She felt Crawford slip a finger deep inside her, and his tongue circled her peak in unison, creating a delicious rhythm. Sadie lifted her head and looked down to see Crawford between her legs, his eyes hard and hot gazing back at her. The tension coiled tighter as she watched him love her between her legs. Her tender bud began to throb uncontrollably beneath his skilled tongue, and her body grew taut. On the very verge of something unknown, Sadie held back until she saw Crawford's tongue flick over her excruciatingly tender flesh.

Her head fell back in surrender, and she cried out. Her body coiled into a tight, hot ball then burst forth, shooting sensation after tingling sensation through her body, down to her toes. Light burst behind her eyes, and energy unlike anything she'd ever experienced raced through her body, making her feel light and weightless.

Crawford watched as Sadie came, his cock throbbing painfully. His heart clutched in his chest as he watched her take the pleasure he had given her. Unable to hold back any longer, the hungry, primitive need to sink deep inside her too much to resist, he positioned himself between her thighs.

The plump head of his erection slid along her slick folds and pushed gently in. Groaning from the hot, wet feel of her, Crawford whispered roughly, "Sadie, I can't wait any longer. I need to be inside you."

Feeling boneless and weak, Sadie only nodded, her body relaxed. Crawford pushed further in until he came to her barrier. His brow furrowed deep in concentration, his body tense, he looked up at Sadie with a mixture of lust and regret in his eyes. Knowing what he was thinking, she shook her head and drew him down for a deep kiss.

Before she sealed her mouth to his, Sadie whispered, "You won't hurt me, Crawford. I want you."

He captured Sadie's mouth with his and, with one strong thrust, buried himself deep inside her. She let out a cry just as Crawford growled deep in his throat.

He held himself deep inside, letting Sadie become accustomed to the feel of his shaft buried in her. Looking into her eyes, Crawford said between gritted teeth, "I'm sorry, love, for hurting you. It's over now, I promise."

Sadie looked into his beautiful blue eyes full of caring and concern and smiled. "It's better now."

Smiling in return, Crawford slowly started to move. "Sadie, lift your legs up, love."

Doing as he bade, Sadie gasped as Crawford slid further inside her. As they rocked together in nature's rhythm, he thrust deep inside and slowly pulled out. Sadie felt tension begin to build again, and thrust up to meet him.

Consumed by passion, Crawford rode her steadily until he felt her begin to writhe beneath him. He then picked up the pace and thrust harder, deeper, faster inside her. His hard body screamed for release, urging him to take more of her.

Lifting Sadie's leg, Crawford draped it around his waist and thrust deep. She moaned, consumed in the throes of passion again. Thrust after thrust, Crawford rode Sadie until he felt her hot sheath tighten around him.

Knowing she was near peak again, he demanded, "Tell me again. I want to hear it. Tell me you want me."

Panting, she wrapped her other leg around Crawford's waist and moaned. Lost in the moment, Sadie didn't hear his demand. Thrusting deep and holding still, he said forcefully, his voice thick with passion, "Tell me, Sadie. I need to hear you say it."

Through eyes hazy with passion, Sadie looked at Crawford, his face hard with tension, his eyes glittering. "I want you. Insatiably. *Always*."

On a throaty groan, Crawford lost control and thrust deep, making Sadie splinter apart. Shards of glittering glass shot out from her core and floated, shimmering in the air, and sent him barreling toward his own release.

CHAPTER FOURTEEN

THE GRAND RHODES Theatre stood tall in the heart of bustling London, its ornate façade a testament to the centuries of artistic endeavors that had unfolded within its hallowed walls. It was a place where dreams were spun into reality and where the magic of the stage transported audiences to far-off lands and whimsical realms. With each step through its gilded entrance, patrons were swept away on a wave of anticipation, ready to be immersed in a world of entertainment like no other.

The moment Sadie set foot in the theatre's opulent foyer the following night, her senses were immediately tantalized. The air was thick with the scent of freshly polished wood and the faint aroma of perfumes worn by the city's fashionable elite. The sound of tinkling laughter and excited chatter danced through the space, creating an infectious buzz of anticipation. On any given night, the theatre's entrance was a bustling scene. Men donned their finest top hats and tails, while women adorned themselves in elegant gowns adorned with feathers and lace. Carriages lined the streets, waiting to transport the theatre's esteemed guests to an evening of pure delight.

Inside the theatre, the atmosphere was electric. Ushers clad in crisp uniforms with gold braiding guided guests to their seats, ensuring everyone had a prime view of the stage. The hum of anticipation was intermingled with the soft rustle of silk and the delicate clinking of champagne glasses. The audience, a vibrant tapestry of characters, awaited the beginning of another extraordinary performance.

The theatre's interior was a sight to behold, a veritable feast for the eyes. Swirling velvet curtains draped elegantly from the ceiling, their deep red hues hinting at the passion and drama that would soon unfold on the stage. Gilded cherubs adorned the walls, their delicate wings seeming to flutter in the soft glow of the chandeliers that cast a warm and inviting light upon the eager audience below.

The orchestra pit, nestled snugly at the foot of the stage, was a hidden world of musicians. Skilled violinists, cellists, and trumpeters tuned their instruments with practiced precision, their melodies floating through the air like whispers of anticipation. The conductor, with his animated gestures, guided the musicians, ensuring that each note played would resonate with the hearts of those in attendance. Sadie loved it. She could see why Rainville owned it—why Carenza performed there. Tonight, she couldn't wait to see her friend perform. She awaited *all* of tonight's performances.

She couldn't wait to see Crawford, either—perhaps most of all. From her vantage point high in the balcony, Sadie watched eagerly for him to appear in the Castleburys' private box. Tonight, she would find a way to be with him again. Had to. Like an addiction.

Only this addiction was laying claim to her heart.

As the lights dimmed and the murmurs of the crowd subsided, the stage burst to life. Lush backdrops painted with meticulous attention to detail transported the audience to exotic lands and enchanted forests. Trapdoors concealed beneath the polished floorboards revealed surprising entrances and dramatic exits, as if the very stage itself possessed a mischievous spirit.

From behind the curtains emerged a cast of colorful characters, each one more vibrant and captivating than the last. The actors, with their impeccable costumes and exaggerated gestures, breathed life into tales of love, treachery, and comedy. The audience was enthralled, their eyes wide with wonder as they were swept away on waves of emotions, their laughter echoing through the theatre like music.

During intermission, patrons mingled in the lavishly decorated corridors, their conversations filled with animated discussions about the performances. The scent of freshly baked pastries wafted from the facility's elegant tearoom, tempting theatregoers to indulge in delicate treats and fine teas. The laughter and chatter grew louder, creating a joyous atmosphere that enveloped the entire building. Sadie tried desperately to catch sight of Crawford, to find him and let him know she was there. However, she missed her opportunity, and intermission ended before she found him.

As the final act approached, the anticipation in the air was palpable. The audience settled back into their plush seats, their hearts racing with anticipation. The stage came alive once more, and the performers poured their hearts and souls into their craft, their voices filling every corner of the theatre. Sadie waited for Crawford to look up, to peer around the theatre to see that she was there. But he didn't. Her heart sank in disappointment.

When the final curtain fell, the theatre erupted in thunderous applause and standing ovations. The air was thick with exhilaration, as if the very walls of the Rhodes Theatre reverberated with the joy and satisfaction of a performance well received.

As the audience reluctantly waited for the next performance, their spirits were uplifted, their souls nourished by the magic they had just witnessed. They milled about the theatre with a twinkle in their eyes, their hearts lightened, and their imaginations ignited.

Rhodes Theatre, a sanctuary of creativity and enchantment, had once again woven its spell, leaving its patrons forever touched by the transformative power of the stage. And so, the grand theatre stood, its doors open wide, ready to welcome the next generation of dreamers and adventurers into its illustrious embrace.

Finally, the curtains rose once more, revealing a stage transformed into a whimsical world where reality blurred with fantasy. Acrobats twirled high above, their bodies defying gravity in a mesmerizing display of strength and agility. A ballet troupe pirouetted gracefully, their movements painting ethereal pictures in the air. And in the center of it all, a spot for the star performer.

Amidst the hushed anticipation of the audience at Rhodes Theatre, a new performance was about to unfold, one that would stir souls and leave hearts breathless. The whispers in the air hinted at a renowned opera singer gracing the illustrious stage, the Masked Meadowlark, her voice said to possess the power to move mountains and touch the heavens themselves.

As the audience settled into their plush seats, a wave of excitement washed over the theatre. The lights dimmed, and a hush fell upon the crowd, like the calm before a tempest. A lone spotlight pierced the darkness, illuminating the stage where the diva would soon stand.

And there she appeared, a vision of grace and elegance, adorned in a resplendent gown that shimmered like moonlit waters. Her entrance alone commanded attention, every eye fixed upon her, every heart skipping a beat. She exuded an aura of timeless beauty, a presence that demanded reverence. Sadie's best friend, Carenza. Crawford's sister.

With a nod to the conductor, the orchestra began to play, their instruments intertwining in a symphony of anticipation. The familiar strains of the overture caressed the air, setting the stage for the grand opera that was about to unfold. And then, with a surge of emotion, the diva's voice soared, filling the vast expanse of the theatre.

Her voice, a celestial instrument, painted vivid tapestries of love, longing, and heartache. It carried the weight of centuries of human emotion, each note a brush stroke on the canvas of the audience's souls. From delicate trills to commanding crescendos, her range knew no bounds, traversing octaves effortlessly, captivating all who had the privilege of listening.

The audience sat transfixed, their eyes locked upon the exquisite figure before them. Her voice resonated with such power and clarity that it seemed to penetrate every heart, leaving no emotion untouched. It was as if she wove invisible threads, connecting each member of the audience to the heartache, joy, and passion of the character she portrayed.

Her every movement was a dance, choreographed with precision and grace. She moved with the fluidity of a swan, her gestures accentuating the emotion in every word she sang. Her expressive eyes mirrored the depths of her characters' souls, conveying longing, despair, and ecstasy with a single glance.

As the aria reached its climactic peak, the theatre held its breath. The Meadowlark's voice soared to unimaginable heights, a cascade of sound that reverberated through the very bones of the building. It was a moment suspended in time, where the boundary between performer and audience dissolved, and all were united in the pure magic of her art.

And then, as the final notes lingered in the air, the theatre erupted in rapturous applause. The audience rose as one, their ovation a testament to the awe and wonder that had enveloped them. Tears glistened in the eyes of many, their hearts overflowing with the sheer beauty and emotional depth of the performance they had witnessed.

The Masked Meadowlark took her well-deserved bows, her radiant smile a reflection of the joy she had brought to others.

Sadie, once again, had witnessed a performance for the ages, a night where an opera singer who happened to be her best friend had become a vessel for the dreams and emotions of an enraptured audience. It was a night that would forever be etched in the memories of those lucky enough to be in attendance.

She glanced down once again to where Crawford sat, and her heart jolted when they made eye contact. His blue eyes flared like an inferno, even from the distance. She smiled softly, enticingly.

He nodded, a small, stiff gesture, looking so very proper in his evening attire. Sadie wondered what it would be like to sit next to him in that box. To be his duchess and his wife. To step out into the world as who she really was, not a shadow of herself hiding in a plain dress in a balcony seat reserved for those of no importance and little means.

Crawford caught her eye with a nod toward the entrance. And somehow, she knew. She knew what he wanted and where he wanted it.

Her feet were moving before she'd drawn a full breath, heading toward the curtained alcove she had passed earlier. Growing breathless with every step, the thrill and anticipation urging her on, Sadie stepped down the hall.

And found him waiting.

HIS HANDS WERE everywhere the second the large velvet alcove curtain closed behind them. He had to touch her. If he didn't, he'd go insane. Blast it, he already felt insane these days. For Sadie. Completely and utterly for Sadie and her goddamned beautiful arse. Every time he blinked he saw her juicy backside showcased in those damned trousers she wore, and lust slapped him like a strumpet denied her hard-earned coin.

They stumbled together in the dark alcove. Crawford tore his lips from her as they slammed into a plant stand. "I can't see. Shite, I can't see a goddamn thing back here." He tried to find the curtain against the wall to pull it ajar just slightly—enough to see her in the dark. Her shape, her silhouette—anything.

He felt her hands race over him in the dark, searching until she found his hand. She grabbed it and placed it on her bodice. "Use your hands and feel your way, my lord."

"*Selkie.*" The air rushed from his lungs.

Her other hand stroked up his stomach, and she tore at his waistcoat and tunic shirt. Buttons popped open, and her mouth was on his throat in a wildly uninhibited kiss. Her tongue traced his skin, burning a path down his chest.

His heart fell, dove right into love, and flopped at her feet.

"Mine," he growled, knowing in his soul that she belonged with him.

He grabbed her hip and walked backward to where he vaguely recalled a bench. She tripped, and instantly they plummeted to the ground. Reacting instantly, Crawford turned until he cradled her in his protective arms, and hit the theatre alcove floor first. She plopped and sprawled on top of him. His breath left him in a rush, and he grunted. Sadie draped herself across his chest, her own rush of air whooshing from her.

Then she was giggling in the most delightful way.

"Pray tell, what's so amusing?" he rasped, his heart stuttering with so much feeling for this woman.

"Apparently I've gone and tumbled for you, Crawford. Tumbled us both."

A rush of heat pooled in his gut, twisting it in a tight knot. God, could it be true? He suddenly wanted Sadie to fall for him in the worst way. The thought of it set his heart racing.

Clearly they had secrets from one another. But he'd be a blasted liar if he said he didn't want Sadie to fall for him. Because he wanted it fiercely. *Desperately.* Like a bloody fool, he had gone and fallen for her. Tumble, he most certainly had.

She slid over him until she was straddling him on the marble floor in the dark. He could barely make out her silhouette in the near blackness. But he could feel her. *How* he could feel her. Her heat, the weight of her, the hands that seared a path down his bare chest. And it turned his cock to stone.

"I've wanted to do this, wanted to run my hands all over your hard body again. I've dreamt of it at night and fantasized about it during the daylight hours." Her voice sounded husky with arousal. It brushed over him like velvet and settled in his loins.

He tried to reach for her, but she stopped him. "Let me touch you, Sadie. Let me kiss and lick every inch of your luscious body. I'm half crazed with want for you. Once wasn't enough. Nothing will ever be enough. Come here." He reached for her again.

He growled when she stopped his hands. She pushed them to the floor with a tsk. "Uh-uh. My way this time, earl. Now lie there like a good lad and keep your hands to yourself until I tell you otherwise."

"No," he growled again.

"Oh yes," she countered, laughing gently.

He needed inside her soon, or he was going to lose all control and take her hard. Or come in his trousers. "I can't wait any longer. I want to be in you." Her fingers skimmed low over his stomach, and he hissed, *"Now,* Sadie."

She reached his trouser buttons and pressed her hand over his erection. She sounded amused when she tsked some more. "My, my, aren't you in a hurry?" She stroked him through his trousers "I thought earls were trained to maintain all discipline."

He rocked against her hand. A groan ripped from his throat as she caressed him with her small, surprisingly strong hand. "Another time. I'll be disciplined later. Right now, I need to feel you around me. Damn it, if you don't stop stroking my cock, I won't even make it long enough to thrust into your beautiful pussy."

His breathing grew absolutely ragged. He was attuned to Sadie's every movement in the darkness of the theatre alcove. Electricity skittered along his skin, his senses heightened to an almost painful alert and tuned completely to her. When she undid his trouser flap and took him in her hands, it was almost too much to bear. He arched helplessly upward and ground out, "Yes."

"Oh, do you like that?" She ran her palm up his cock and gripped him. She slid her thumb over the head and rubbed a bead of moisture into the sensitive flesh, and he nearly lost control then and there. Sadie moved over him, and he heard rustling, could tell she was removing her clothing. Unable to resist anymore, he reached for her and slid his hands over her hot, bare skin.

He had never felt like this for any woman before—like a wild animal. Something primitive tore through Crawford as he squeezed her perfect breasts and she moaned. He flicked the pad of his thumb over her tightly budded nipples. There was a sharp tug low in his stomach, and his cock ached so badly it throbbed. It was pleasure and pain, heaven and hell—and he never wished it to end.

"Crawford, kiss me," Sadie demanded in a rough whisper.

He sat up and ran his hands over her body to fist her short, silky hair. A growl rumbled deep in his chest when his hungry mouth found hers in the dark and he fed her a scorching, deep kiss. She moaned, a helpless sound, and he smiled wickedly against her lips. Loving the sound, he yanked her head back and trailed impatient kisses down her throat. She arched against him as his mouth roughly covered her breast and he sucked her taut peak.

He held her in place as he tongued her hard bud and cupped her other breast. They were perfect, firm and ripe and sweet. He wanted to devour every inch of her like a ravaging beast.

At that moment, it didn't matter that Sadie was in hiding and that he still had no idea why. All that he cared about was her ragged moans and the nails that dug into his back, telling him she wanted him. That she was wet and ready for him.

But something else first.

SADIE FELT CRAWFORD'S toned body flex, the sculpted muscles bunch, and then she was flat on her back on the alcove floor, the smooth marble tiles cold against her shoulders. He loomed over her in the darkness, his hard length rubbing against her core. She gave a throaty groan when he shoved roughly against her, brushing her swollen bud with his silken tip. It might have hurt if she wasn't so aroused. Instead, tremors shot off inside her like fireworks.

"Now you're in trouble, Selkie. You're going to pay for teasing me," Crawford growled against her throat.

She damned well hoped so.

Power swam in her blood like an elixir. She'd made Crawford hard, lustful for her. Her. Sadie Crisp. The knowledge went straight to her head like brandy.

Knowing she affected him meant everything, because she was falling for the earl with the thick thighs and incredible hands. It mattered not that it was the most foolish thing she could possibly do, or that it ruined all her plans. She couldn't stop it, any more than England could cease raining in January.

A gasp escaped her when Crawford's hand streaked up her skirts and dove inside. Through her drawers he touched her.

"You're so wet, Sadie. Your drawers are soaked with your desire for me. I can smell it on you. But I need to hear you say it. Tell me how you feel," he commanded.

In the darkness behind the theatre curtain, lying on the marble floor, she felt his fingers stroke her through her drawers, and she groaned. He pushed a finger around the soft, aged cotton and found her damp, aching center, touching her exactly where she craved him the most.

"Say it, Sadie. Tell me that your gorgeous little quim is wet for me." His lips found a sensitive spot below her ear, and he kissed her there. His tongue glided over the curve of her ear, and he nipped her playfully. She gasped and rocked into his fingers.

"I'm so wet, Crawford," she rasped, and her center went molten. Could she burst into flames?

His mouth trailed a searing path down her chest. His tongue flicked over the tight peaks of her nipples before he continued on his path. "No," he grunted against her stomach, "tell me that I make you wet. That I make you ache. Say those very words, Sadie. It arouses me more than you could possibly know, hearing your sweet, pretty mouth say such naughty things."

Good God, she *liked* his dirty talk, and her body responded to the earthiness of it, the baseness of this side of him.

Sadie unleashed. "I ache for you, Crawford. This deep, thrumming ache between my thighs. I'm so wet, and it's all your fault. Only you can fix it." It was true. Crawford was exactly what she needed. The *only* thing.

His rough, sharp laugh echoed in the small alcove. Yanking his hand from her drawers, he ripped them off, tearing them at the seams. He left her for a moment, and she heard him strip his trousers off. Then he returned, and his hard, strong hands ran up the length of her bare thighs.

He traced a finger over her damp curls at her center. "Only I can fix it. Remember that, Selkie. But I'll not ease your ache yet, Sadie. You teased me—now it's my turn. Ask me if I want to kiss your quim."

Sadie reached for him, touched him everywhere she could reach. Arms, shoulders, the back of his head. He blew on her woman's mound, and her body caught fire.

She gave him what he wanted to hear, lost to any and all sense of propriety. "Want to kiss my quim, Crawford? The one that's dripping for you?"

His answer was fast and hard. *"Yes."*

Then his mouth took her core in a hot, consuming kiss, lapping at her, tasting her. A sound of primitive arousal tore from his throat. He found her swollen nub with his tongue, stroked over it, and sucked roughly, possessively. Sadie thought she might die from the delicious, overwhelming thrill of it.

When her inner muscles started to clench around his talented fingers, Crawford moved. His athletic body covered her, and the thick, plump head of his manhood pushed insistently between her slick and swollen folds.

Hunger clawed deep in her core, and she arched her hips. On a vicious curse, he sank into her, groaning deeply. He stretched her wide, and she gasped.

He thrust deep, and her inner muscles clamped around him, started to quiver. "That's my girl," he encouraged her. "Come for me."

When he kissed her, she tasted herself on his lips. His tongue dueled with hers as he began moving in aggravatingly slow strokes.

Sadie didn't want slow. She raised her legs and wrapped them around Crawford's muscular shoulders, taking him deeper still, feeling him against her womb.

Nothing else in the world existed. Only her, and only Crawford.

"Give me more." She nipped his neck, and he swore darkly.

"More?" he ground out, the sound harsh.

"Yes!" She scored her nails along his arms. *"Now."*

He gave it to her, rutting into her harder, faster, pounding. He kept the unrelenting pace until her desire became a white-hot ball of need in her core. Until she could only feel and cling helplessly to Crawford.

Again and again he thrust into her until she cried out in the darkness, her body bursting into a thousand tiny, sparkling shards. Her climax tore through her with so much force that tears sprang to her eyes. She held to him, convulsed around him, until he rutted deep, a groan ripped from his chest, and he went rigid with his own climax.

CHAPTER FIFTEEN

"Y OU LOOK CHIPPER," West commented with a questioning look in his gray eyes as he pulled an ale from the tap and sent it sliding down the glossy, scarred bar top. Due to word of a secret appearance by London's vocal darling, the Masked Meadowlark, the pub was packed to the beams with those eager to hear her sensational voice ringing out once more in the local establishment. These days, Rhodes Theatre was her preferred venue for performing.

"Am," Sadie replied with a shrug of one shoulder. As if her happiness wasn't a big deal.

Dear heavens, Crawford made her *happy*. The blasted *timing* of it all.

Her. *Happy*.

"And here I'd thought it could no longer exist for me."

"What was that?" the pub owner asked, his back to her as he served a dockworker the largest mug of ale Sadie had ever seen.

"What did you do, use your boot as a cast for that mug?" Sadie tipped her chin at the towering glass of ale.

West laughed, a deep rumble in his barrel chest. "Maybe."

"What are you two going on about?"

Sadie turned with a ready smile on her lips, recognizing the voice of Viscount Amslee. "Carenza didn't say you'd be here tonight."

"Change of plans," Damon said, his dark eyes taking in the

crowd. "I don't like her singing without my watching guard."

"Revivalists won't get to her again, mate." West's lips compressed into a grim, determined line. "I promise."

"You've already done enough on that front, O'Connell. You nearly sacrificed a kidney." The viscount turned his intense scrutiny onto Sadie. Fortunately, she was used to it. "You too."

"Aw, thanks, you tender heart." Sadie grinned at Damon's fleeting grimace. "I'll be sure to keep my kidneys intact, just for you," she quipped, her tone light despite the lingering weight of her thoughts.

Damon chuckled, a smile spreading across his rugged features. "Glad to hear it. We wouldn't want to lose our favorite troublemaker, now, would we?"

West leaned in closer, his gray eyes twinkling with mischief. "Speaking of trouble, have you heard the latest gossip about Viscountess Beecham? I swear, that woman's antics never cease to amaze me."

Sadie laughed, eager for the distraction. As Damon and West launched into a lively discussion about the scandalous exploits of London's High Society, she couldn't help but feel a sense of camaraderie wash over her. Despite the chaos of her own life, there was comfort to be found in the familiar banter of her friends. But even as she laughed and joked with them, Sadie couldn't shake the image of Crawford from her mind. His piercing gaze, the strength of his hands as they worked their magic on her body and soul—it all seemed to linger like a tantalizing promise of something more.

With a sigh, Sadie pushed aside her thoughts of Crawford and focused on the present moment. Tonight was about enjoying the music, reveling in the company of her friends, and savoring the simple joys of life—even amidst the turmoil and uncertainty that seemed to follow her wherever she went.

Just then, the Masked Meadowlark made her grand entrance into the tavern, and Sadie felt a mix of awe and envy wash over her. The crowd erupted into applause as Carenza, her best friend and the tavern's beloved singer, graced the stage in her exquisite gown and jeweled mask.

Damon, standing beside Sadie, let out a low growl under his breath, his eyes narrowed as he watched the admiring glances of the other men in the tavern. "Bloody hell," he muttered. "Can't even enjoy a pint without every man in the room ogling my wife."

Sadie couldn't help but chuckle at his grumbling, though her heart twinged with envy at the depth of his love for her friend. Not that she wanted him for herself. She wanted the love. "Oh, Damon," she teased, nudging him playfully with her elbow. "You know you love the attention. Besides, it's not every day we get to hear the Masked Meadowlark grace us with her presence."

The viscount huffed, but a hint of a smile tugged at the corners of his lips. "I suppose you're right," he conceded, his gaze softening as he turned his attention back to the stage. "But that doesn't mean I have to like it."

Sadie grinned. "No, I suppose not," she agreed, her eyes lingering on her friend as she began to sing. "But you have to admit, she's absolutely captivating up there."

And as Carenza's voice filled the tavern, weaving a spellbinding melody that seemed to transport them all to another world, Sadie couldn't help but feel a sense of awe wash over her. Despite her envy, there was no denying the magic of her friend's performance, and she found herself swept away by the beauty of the moment.

As the final notes of Carenza's haunting melody faded into the air, Damon leaned down beside her, his voice low and serious as he whispered in her ear. "Sadie," he said, his tone causing a shiver along her skin, "I'm worried about you. There are rumors circulating that your cousin has tripled his efforts to find you. He's even offering a reward to anyone who can bring you to him."

Sadie's blood ran cold at his words, her heart pounding with fear at the thought of her cousin's relentless pursuit. She knew all too well the lengths Archibald would go to in order to claim her fortune, and the idea of his closing in on her sent panic slicing through her. "Tripled his efforts?" she echoed, her voice barely above a whisper as she turned to face her friend. Her heart raced as Damon's words sank in. "He must know I'm still in London," she murmured, her voice trembling with fear. "But how? I've been so careful."

The viscount's expression softened with concern as he reached out to grasp Sadie's hand in his own. "I don't know," he admitted. "But we need to find a way to keep you safe. Is there anywhere else you can go? Somewhere he wouldn't think to look?"

Sadie shook her head, her mind racing as she struggled to think of a solution. "No," she whispered, her voice barely audible over the din of the tavern. "I've already exhausted all my options. There's nowhere else for me to go."

Damon's brow furrowed with worry as he squeezed Sadie's hand reassuringly, like a good and trusted friend. "We'll figure something out," he vowed, his dark gaze unwavering. "I promise we won't let anything happen to you. Will we, West?"

"Nope. I told you I'm here when you need me. Meant it."

Sadie forced a weak smile, grateful for their unwavering support. "Thank you." She knew that time was running out, and that she would have to find a way to outsmart Cousin Archibald if she hoped to stay one step ahead.

Her thoughts drifted back to Crawford, her heart yearning for the safety and comfort she felt in his presence. She imagined what it would be like to confide in him, to share her fears and her truths, and to feel the warmth of his embrace enveloping her in a cocoon of protection.

As the men's reassuring words washed over her, she felt a surge of determination well up inside her. "I need to tell Crawford the truth about me, don't I?" she said, her voice pitched over the din of the tavern.

Damon nodded curtly. "Yes, Sadie," he replied. "You do.

You're not alone anymore. You have people who care about you, who will fight to protect you. He deserves to be given that chance."

She knew she couldn't continue to carry the burden of her fears alone, and that she needed to lean on those who cared for her most. "I'm grateful for you all," she murmured, her voice suddenly choked with emotion.

Damon was right, and she knew she needed to have a serious conversation with Crawford, but for the moment, she very much needed to lighten the mood. "Speaking of significant others," she began, her tone light and teasing as she turned to Carenza's husband, "does your manservant Bones have one? My landlord seemed quite taken with him when he dropped the missive by the other day."

The viscount chuckled at Sadie's playful deflection. "Ah, Bones," he replied, shaking his head fondly. "No, he hasn't been with anyone since his wife passed. She was taken by the Revivalists, and he's never quite been the same since."

Sadie's heart ached at the mention of Bones's loss. "That's heartbreaking," she murmured.

Damon nodded. "It is," he agreed. "But I can't help but think that meeting someone new might be just what the old bugger needs." He glanced down at her. "Your landlord, eh?"

"German widow, always prying in my affairs, big heart, loves to cook." How else did one describe Frau Olsen?

"Excellent." Damon grinned devilishly. "That's *exactly* what he needs."

"Hey now," West called out from behind the bar, his eyes flickering faintly with panic as he looked back and forth between the two of them. "Don't go matching up everyone you know, you hear?"

"Yes, West." Sadie chuckled agreeably, enjoying his clear discomfort.

"I'm serious," he nearly yelled, polishing the taps frantically now.

"Understood," she agreed with a jaunty nod. Serious, indeed.

"Damn it, you two better keep your noses out of things."

"Calm down," Damon drawled, raking his eyes over the bartender. "You look ready to faint."

"Love," the bartender muttered, turning his attention to scrubbing a nonexistent spot on the bar top. "It's like a damn disease around here."

CHAPTER SIXTEEN

THE GAS LAMPS flickered with an eerie glow the following night, casting a hazy light over the myriad alleys of the London Docks as Crawford strode down them. A thick, swirling fog wrapped around the masts of the docked ships, shrouding them in an otherworldly veil. The scent of damp wood and briny sea hung heavy in the air, mingling with the distant cries of seagulls and the clattering of horse-drawn carriages on cobblestone streets.

As the evening descended into darkness, the fog grew thicker, transforming the docks into a mysterious realm where shadows danced and whispered secrets. Gasps of misty breath escaped the lips of figures clad in top hats and long coats, their faces hidden beneath the cover of fog. Men and women scurried about, their footsteps muffled by the dampness underfoot, clutching tightly to parcels and satchels as they hurriedly made their way through the labyrinthine streets.

Every now and then, the piercing sound of a distant foghorn broke through the stillness, its mournful cry echoing across the foggy expanse like a ghostly wail. It sent a shiver down the spines of those who dared venture into the murky night, their hearts racing with a mix of trepidation and excitement. Hell, it sent a shiver down Crawford's spine. The flickering gas lamps, their glass panes encrusted with dew, provided mere glimpses into the inky darkness, teasing his imagination with fleeting shapes and ethereal forms.

Amidst the thrill and mystique of the foggy night, a palpable sense of unease lurked in the air—he could feel it. Sense it. The fog possessed an almost sentient quality, twisting and curling around unsuspecting passersby, obscuring his vision and distorting reality. Whispers of ghostly apparitions and eerie creatures prowling the docks abounded in his mind, tales of phantom sailors and lost souls who found no rest. Everywhere he looked, his imagination leapt to life.

The fog played tricks on his senses, distorting the perception of time and space. Familiar landmarks seemed to shift and morph, leading even the most seasoned Londoner astray—himself included. It was a night where caution and curiosity danced a delicate waltz, and the line between reality and fantasy blurred into a hauntingly enchanting spectacle.

Everything had felt blurry and enchanting since he'd had a taste of Sadie.

As the clock ticked closer to midnight, the fog clung ever tighter, wrapping the London Docks in its ethereal embrace. Shadows stretched and elongated, taking on monstrous forms in his mind's eye. The air grew colder, the atmosphere thick with anticipation and a touch of dread.

Perhaps it was because everything had changed for him, but in the foggy night at the London Docks, he could not help but feel a sense of adventure tinged with a hint of danger, as if something was out there ready to take hold of unwary souls who dared to wander too far into the shadowy depths of the docks.

"Could be the bloody shark," he muttered, unease skittering down his back. "Could be that it's back."

Within the swirling fog, the sound of creaking wood and rustling sails of the ships were carried on the damp breeze. It was as if the very essence of the docks was awakening, a symphony of haunting notes played upon invisible strings. The shifting fog seemed to part for a moment, revealing the ghostly outline of a towering ship, its masts reaching toward the heavens like skeletal fingers as he made his way down the quay. The vessel loomed like a phantom from another time, its worn hull bearing the scars of countless voyages.

From the heart of the Commercial Docks, the distant clatter of chains and the muffled thud of crates being loaded onto ships whispered of untold stories as he passed. Crawford's curiosity begged to be satisfied, drawing him closer to the source of those mysterious sounds. The narrow alleyways off the quay beckoned him, their cobblestones worn with the footsteps of sailors long gone.

As Crawford ventured deeper into the dock, a flickering gas lamp illuminated a weathered sign swinging gently in the misty breeze. It read *The Haunted Mermaid Tavern*. The inviting warmth of the pub spilled out onto the fog-laden street, accompanied by the boisterous laughter of patrons and the clinking of tankards. It was a haven for sailors, a sanctuary where tales of the supernatural mingled with the hearty scent of ale and tobacco smoke. He thought of Sadie, wondered how often she had a pint there after her shift ended. Lured by the thought, he opened the door.

Inside, the air was thick with the lingering echoes of ghostly legends. Weathered men with salt-crusted beards leaned against the bar, their eyes filled with both reverence and trepidation as they shared tales of sea monsters and mermaids. The flickering fire cast dancing shadows upon the walls, bringing to life the stories whispered among the dockworkers and deal porters. Crawford stood there for several minutes, envisioning Sadie's life, her experiences. His heart swelled in his chest, knowing that only a woman of truly exceptional spirit could do what she did.

Sadie Crisp was one hell of a woman.

Back outside the tavern, the fog swirled in eddies, as if listening to the tales being spun within. Shadows moved and merged, assuming eerie forms that hinted at the presence of unseen beings. Whispers of disembodied voices floated through the mist, carrying tales of lost souls and forbidden love. The streets seemed alive, vibrating with a strange energy that set Crawford's skin prickling.

Perhaps it was his imagination. Perhaps it was the Revivalists. Or perhaps it was merely the blasted shark.

Amidst the ambience, an old street peddler with a mischievous glint in his eye offered Crawford trinkets and charms said to ward off evil spirits. The wrinkled man claimed to possess relics from far-off lands, each with a story woven into its very fabric. The skeptic in Crawford scoffed, but he again thought of Sadie and couldn't resist purchasing a talisman or two, seeking protection for her against the unseen forces that prowled London. As he picked them out, he listened to the tale told by the peddler. A tale of a Spanish galleon...

Once upon a time, amidst the sparkling cerulean waters of the vast ocean, there sailed a magnificent wooden Spanish galleon—a ship straight out of the pages of a historical romance novel. A vessel that embodied the very essence of adventure, romance, and irresistible allure of the high seas.

This enchanting beauty was a flirtatious temptress, with a curvaceous figure that effortlessly glided through the water like a graceful dancer. Her towering masts, tall and proud, reached for the heavens, adorned with billowing sails that caught the wind's gentle caress and carried her on her thrilling journey.

Her wooden frame, weathered and kissed by the sun, told tales of countless escapades on distant shores. Each plank seemed to hold a whispered secret, a forgotten rendezvous, or a stolen kiss in the moonlight. Her scent was a delightful mix of saltwater, adventure, and dreams yet to be realized, inviting all who encountered her to join her whimsical world.

Oh, the details! The galleon's hull boasted intricate carvings, painstakingly etched by skilled craftsmen. Delicate figures of mermaids, their tails elegantly entwined, seemed to come alive as they danced along the ship's sides, their laughter echoing through the waves. And atop the bow, a splendidly carved figurehead—a fearless lion, his mane flowing in the wind—gazed boldly into the horizon, as if daring destiny to bring forth new encounters and tales of passion.

The ship's deck was a lively tapestry of vibrant colors, lined with barrels of rum and crates of exotic treasures. There, a crew bustled about, their laughter mingling with the rhythmic sound of the waves. Sailors in breeches and open shirts, their sun-kissed skin shimmering, worked in harmony as they prepared for their next escapade, their playful banter floating through the air like a mischievous melody.

Onboard, a captain of undeniable charm and charisma led his merry band of seafarers. With a twinkle in his eye and a rakish grin, he possessed an air of mystery that made hearts skip a beat. His velvet voice, like the gentle lapping of waves against the shore, carried his orders across the ship, and his crew willingly followed, captivated by his infectious spirit.

As the galleon sailed into the golden sunset, the distant shores beckoned, promising uncharted lands, hidden treasures, and enchanting encounters. The ship and its crew, fueled by a thirst for adventure, reveled in the unknown, guided by the stars above and the winds that whispered sweet secrets through their sails.

When the peddler finished his tale, Crawford thanked him and continued on to his destination—his very own Spanish galleon that went by the name of *Susanna's Secret*.

The ship's hull, strong and resolute, bore the marks of countless adventures upon its weathered surface. Its timeworn planks, lovingly carved by skilled hands, recounted tales of distant lands and intrepid explorations. Each groove and knot told a story, whispering of past triumphs, devastating storms, and daring escapades that defied the imagination.

Oh, the details that adorned this majestic ship his father so loved. Exquisite carvings of mythical creatures, fearsome dragons, and majestic sea serpents decorated the stern, while intricate patterns wound their way along the sides. These intricate embellishments, meticulously etched by master craftsmen, paid homage to the rich heritage of Spain, infusing the vessel with an air of grandeur and nobility.

Crawford could picture the captain, a stalwart figure standing at the helm, his gaze fixed upon the horizon with a mix of determination and curiosity. His weathered face told tales of countless battles and the wisdom gained from traversing uncharted waters. He would have been clad in a splendid uniform, adorned with gleaming buttons and golden epaulets, exuding authority and commanding the respect of his loyal crew.

As the galleon sailed forward across the water, guided by the stars and the salty breeze, a sense of wonder and excitement would have filled the air. The distant shores would have beckoned to the captain, promising untold treasures and unimaginable encounters with foreign lands. The crew, a weathered band of adventurers, would have eagerly anticipated the unknown, their hearts brimming with anticipation for the mysteries that lay ahead.

In the golden light of the setting sun, the ship became a silhouette against the backdrop of the London sky. It reminded Crawford that within the pages of history, there were stories waiting to be discovered, tales of bravery, romance, and the indomitable spirit of those who dared to venture beyond the boundaries of the known world.

What did *he* dare?

The question replayed over and over in his mind as he wound his way through rigging and barrels. Did he dare run this company the very best he could? Did he dare be the best earl he could be?

Did he dare love a woman for the sake of love? Against all societal acceptance and rules?

What *exactly* did Crawford Hunnewell Castlebury want?

Excellent bloody question.

Within the heart of *Susanna's Secret*, tucked away from the bustling deck and the salty sea breeze, was the captain's quarters—a sanctuary that embodied a perfect balance of regality and comfort. Crawford peeked inside, and his senses were swept away by the ambience of the extraordinary space.

He pushed the door open with a creak, revealing a room adorned with rich mahogany woodwork that gleamed softly in the glow of flickering candlelight. Several candles were lit around the chamber, casting a warm golden hue upon the room, illuminating the grandeur within. The air was saturated with the heavy fragrance of sandalwood, creating an atmosphere of tranquility that was both inviting and regal.

At the center of the chamber, a grand four-poster bed stood proudly, draped with opulent curtains that cascaded like waves of silk. The sheets, as soft as a gentle caress, invited his weary body to find solace and rejuvenation. The pillows, plump and inviting, promised dreams as magnificent as the adventures that lay beyond the ship's bow. And he could see himself lying there with Sadie, naked limbs tangling lazily. A sense of rightness filled him at the thought.

Nearby, a polished writing desk stood anchored to the floor and adorned with an assortment of maps, navigational tools, and an intricately crafted compass. Quills and inkwells, poised for inspiration, no doubt beckoned the captain to capture his thoughts, dreams, and secrets within the pages. The desk served as a sanctuary for reflection and planning, where the captain contemplated the ship's course and what possible troubles could await.

Against one wall, a bookshelf showcased a collection of well-worn tomes—tales of exploration, love, and the exploits of fearless adventurers who had trodden the paths before. The captain's thirst for knowledge and the written word was evident in the curated selection, offering a glimpse into the depths of his curiosity and the desire to understand the world that unfolded beyond the ship's wooden embrace.

In a corner of the room, an elegant vanity table snagged his attention. Adorned with a gilded mirror and a delicate porcelain brush set, it served as a private sanctuary for moments of self-indulgence. Perfumes and oils, crafted from exotic flowers and spices, sat gracefully upon the surface, whispering stories of far-off lands and memories waiting to be made. That they too belonged to the ship's captain had Crawford quirking a brow in curiosity. He personally preferred a much simpler hygiene routine.

As he roamed about the quarters, Crawford's mind filled with thoughts of Sadie and his life as earl. "I wish things were different."

Suddenly pain exploded in the back of Crawford's head and his knees buckled. He grunted and dropped to the ground, grabbing his head.

"You pig bastard!" a gruff voice snarled from behind him. "You tainted what belonged to another. Now you're going to pay for it."

His head throbbing, Crawford tried to look back at who had attacked him. "What do you mean? Is this about a shipment of goods?"

"Quiet!"

More pain in the back of his head. Sharp, splintering.

"I don't understand!" he yelled out, desperate to turn around toward his attacker. Or shift his position at all. Any movement and he could turn this to his advantage, use the skills Chai had taught him. "What belonged to another?"

"*Her.*"

Crawford could hear the movement behind him this time and anticipated it, bringing his fist up and into the underside of his attacker's jaw. "Do you mean Sadie?"

"If that's what that bitch calls herself," snarled the man. "She's my property, not yours. You're going to pay for trying to ruin my plans."

"Not tonight, I won't." Crawford sprang, his moment to act arriving. In a few concise moves, he dropped the intruder unconscious to the floor.

Sadie belonged to another man? His mind ranted in disbelief. It couldn't be. That meant Crawford slept with a married woman.

His blood went cold.

Good Christ, was Sadie *married*? Pain sliced through him at the thought. Was *that* why she was in hiding?

There was only one way to know.

Crawford had to confront her.

Rubbing at the budding bump on his head, he set off to find her and get some answers.

CHAPTER SEVENTEEN

"ARE YOU MARRIED?"

Sadie whipped her head up from the stack of papers she was poring over. Seated in Crawford's chair behind his desk, she leapt from it, sending it toppling. "What are you talking about?" She narrowed her eyes on him, and her heart began to pound. "Why would you ask me such a thing?" She noticed his rumpled appearance and disheveled hair, his hot scowl. "Whatever is the matter with you?"

"I was attacked on *Susanna's Secret* in the captain's quarters by a man claiming you belong to him." He raised a brow, his eyes hard and suspicious. Her heart sank seeing it. "Care to explain why, Sadie?"

The blood drained from her head, and she swayed, lightheaded. "Oh no," she whispered. "Oh no, oh no."

"It's true, then?" His pale blue eyes went cold. "You belong to another."

"Yes," she admitted through dry, brittle lips. She'd known this moment would come. Knew in her heart that it had to at some point. Truth always came out.

The bright explosion of pain radiating behind his eyes shook her to her core. "It's not what you think," she rushed to add.

"What I think is that this man who attacked me actually had the right. You're his property. What in God's name were you thinking, Sadie?" His voice rose with the question. "You're *married!"*

"I am *not* married!" she yelled back, getting angry now. "Stop accusing me of infidelity!" *Oh, men. So infuriating.* "I am his ward!" Sadie spat, hating the word. "This man who attacked you is my Cousin Archibald."

"Why is he your guardian, pray tell?"

"Because…" she started, her shoulders slumping. It was time to tell the whole truth. "I am not really a dockworker."

"Shocking revelation," he drawled, dripping sarcasm. His arms were firmly crossed over his chest. "Who are you?"

Sadie took a deep breath and blurted out the truth, part of her thankful to finally get it out there. She had never liked it there between them anyway. "I am the daughter of the Duke and Duchess of Seawell, and the newly titled Duchess of Seawell, Sadie Windcrisp."

"Wait," Crawford said, going very still. "You are Harmon's daughter?"

She swallowed around the lump of tears lodged in her throat. "I am."

"But I don't understand." He took a step toward her. "You're in hiding. Why?"

"Because Cousin Archibald tried to kill me!" She still couldn't believe it. Well, she could. But couldn't. "He put poison in my tea so that he could gain my title and inheritance for himself! I survived and ran away. Hid. I've been hiding for over a year now, looking over my shoulder, praying every night for one more day of safety. But he's coming for me. He'll always come for me. Because as soon as I marry, everything goes to my husband and he keeps nothing. My father already denied him my hand, so he tried to take it. End it. End *me*. I'm not safe as long as he's alive. He'll never stop searching for me."

"You should have told me, Sadie." His voice was soft, low. "You should have told me from the beginning when I asked. Hell," he said in a firmer voice, emotion infusing his tone, "I would have married you weeks ago, given you protection."

Hope burst in her chest, and she looked at him wide-eyed. "You would have?"

He nodded.

"Why?" she asked, coming around the desk to him. She stopped before him and tipped her head back to look up at his gorgeous eyes. "Why would you do such a thing for me?"

"Because," he murmured, reaching for her and pulling her close, "I love you."

Just then, an explosion shook the docks, the floor beneath their feet trembling from the force of it.

"What the devil was that?" Crawford hollered, racing to the window to look outside. Sadie rushed to his side. What she saw chilled her.

Outside, fire raged.

The docklands were burning.

IT BEGAN WITH a flicker, an innocent flame that soon grew into a hungry inferno.

The flames licked at the timber around them, devouring it with a voracious appetite. The fire surged skyward, casting an eerie glow over the darkened quay below. Panic spread like wildfire throughout the dock, and the clanging of bells pierced the night as alarm bells sounded their frantic warnings. Men and women ran out onto the quay, their eyes wide with terror and awe.

From the cobbled streets, the crackling blaze transformed the Western Docks into a scene from Sadie's worst nightmare. Orange and red hues danced upon the brick façades of warehouses, illuminating the night with a hellish light. Ash and embers swirled through the air like malevolent spirits, carried by the blistering winds that fanned the flames and pushed them ever forward.

The sound of splintering wood reverberated through the chaos as fiery fingers clawed their way along the piers, embracing everything in their path. Thick plumes of smoke billowed into the sky, blotting out the moon and plunging the city into an eerie darkness. The crackling inferno fed on stacks of crates, devouring their contents with a fervor that defied reason.

Amidst the chaos, brave souls fought valiantly against the encroaching devastation. Fire brigades, their red engines charging through the mazelike streets, unleashed torrents of water upon the writhing flames. Men, their faces smudged with soot, formed human chains, passing buckets of water from hand to hand in a desperate attempt to contain the spreading conflagration. The heat was intense, blistering the skin and scorching the very air they breathed.

A young girl, her voice lost in the roar of the flames, stood atop a balcony, her hair flowing like a fiery cascade as she screamed for help. A fearless sailor, heedless of the dangers that surrounded him, climbed a ladder to reach her, saving her from certain doom just moments before the balcony collapsed into the inferno below.

The night sky glowed with a relentless determination, as if the very heavens themselves were captivated by the spectacle unfolding on the streets below. Spectators, their faces aglow with awe and terror, watched as the Western Docks became a battleground between man and the elements. The crackling of burning timber and the desperate cries of those caught within the inferno mingled with the cheers and gasps of the onlookers. Even they pitched in and helped in whatever way they could.

Susanna's Secret blazed, lighting the sky with orange and red. The Spanish galleon, once a majestic vessel of exploration and conquest, now stood as a towering inferno upon the expanse of the Western Docks. Flames roared with an insatiable hunger, devouring the ancient timbers that had weathered countless storms and sailed uncharted waters. The crackling flames illuminated the night, casting an terrifying glow upon the surrounding waves.

Sadie watched with a sick heart. From afar, the ship resembled a mythical creature of fire and smoke, billowing clouds of blackened soot into the night sky. The once-proud masts, adorned with tattered sails, leaned precariously, threatening to succumb to the merciless blaze. The salty air carried the acrid scent of burning wood, mingling with the tang of saltwater and the distant cries of seagulls.

Amidst the chaos, the crew fought with desperation, their faces etched with determination and fear. Men, their bodies glistening with sweat, scurried across the ship's deck, passing buckets of water hand to hand, their efforts a mere flicker against the raging tempest of fire. The heat was suffocating, searing their lungs and blistering their skin, yet they pressed on, driven by a desire to save their beloved vessel. Crawford was there, working tirelessly.

As the flames danced and leapt, the crackling of burning timbers harmonized with the lapping of waves against the hull. Embers, carried by the wind, spiraled into the night like glowing fireflies, extinguished moments later as they met the unforgiving embrace of the unfathomable ocean. The ship groaned and creaked under the weight of destruction, its once-proud structure now a skeletal frame consumed by the unrelenting fire.

Crawford stood resolute, his voice booming above the crackling symphony of destruction. He barked orders with unwavering authority, his face illuminated by the fiery glow. With every command, the crew and people rallied.

Sparks reached for the heavens, painting an ethereal tapestry against the backdrop of the night. It was a sight both mesmerizing and terrifying. The once-mighty galleon, its hull scorched and its sails reduced to ashes, seemed to fight against its fate, a vessel trapped in a dance with its own demise.

Hours passed in a haze of smoke and sweat, the battle against the consuming fire growing more desperate by the minute. Crawford and the crew, their bodies weary and minds filled with exhaustion, refused to relent. They fought as if their very souls depended on it, their collective will radiating a defiant energy that defied the odds.

And finally, when the night seemed darkest, when all hope appeared lost, the fire began to wane. The flames subsided, their once-fierce intensity replaced by smoldering embers. The ship, scarred and ravaged, but still standing, emerged from the ashes like a phoenix rising from the depths of destruction.

Sadie waited impatiently for Crawford to come to her. In the distance she could see him, covered in soot and ash, his face smeared with streaks of it. All she wanted was him. His arms, his love, his everything. Marry him she would. Nothing would make her happier.

"There you are, filthy whore. Letting another man dip his wick in you."

"Cousin Archibald!" Sadie gasped and spun toward his voice. "Get away from me."

"I'll do whatever I please, harlot. And you're going to pay for running away from me." The look in his black eyes promised pain and retribution.

"No," Sadie said, then shouted, "Crawford! Crawford, help!"

His head whipped up from down the quay, and he roared, "*Sadie!*"

"Damn you!" her cousin spat, and reached for her arm, tried to yank her to him. Sadie went, flinging herself as hard toward him as she could, praying it would make him stumble off balance.

"My life," Sadie snarled as she rammed into him and sent them both flying backward across the quay. "You can't have it!"

Down they went, slamming into the large stones of the quay. Pain burst from Sadie's shoulder, and she cried out and rolled. Archibald loosened his grip, and she took the opportunity and shoved as hard as she could against him.

He went hurling into the water with a splash. "Help!" he cried, throwing his hands about. "I can't swim!" he screamed, thrashing.

Just then, a sleek gray dorsal fin rose from the water near her cousin as he threw himself about in the water. And in the next instant, her cousin disappeared under the water and his thrashing stopped. A dark bloom colored the dock water in the lamplight.

Archibald did not come back up.

Crawford reached her then and yanked her to him. "Sadie!" he panted, running his hands over her. "My God, Sadie! When I saw him behind you, I thought you were gone." He crushed her to him, holding her in an iron embrace. "I love you. Damn it, I love you. I lost years off my life just now."

Sadie hugged him back and snuggled into his embrace, her heart soaring at his confession of love. "I love you too."

"Marry me," he said, his lips trembling against her forehead. "Marry me and let me love you and keep you safe for the rest of your life."

It was everything she wanted.

"I'll marry you," she replied, smiling against his chest. "So long as you're willing to marry a duchess."

"Dockworker or duchess, you're the woman I want. The woman I love." Crawford lowered his lips to hers gently. "Now, let's get you home."

Sadie glanced at the water, noted the stillness and the inky patch bleeding across the surface. She really could go home.

"It just so happens," she said, smiling, thankful for this wonderful turn of events, "that I have a lovely little townhouse on Park Lane."

"Then take *me* home, Duchess."

She wanted nothing more.

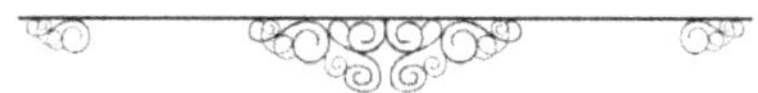

EPILOGUE

Three months later...

THE GOLDEN HUES of autumn enveloped Hyde Park, as if nature had taken out her most enchanting paintbrushes and splashed the world with warmth and radiance. On this glorious fall day, Lady Sadie and Lord Crawford found themselves wandering hand in hand along the meandering paths, their hearts fluttering like the leaves that gently twirled in the breeze.

The sun beamed down from a cloudless sky, casting a playful glow upon the scene. Sadie's eyes sparkled like the diamonds that adorned her dainty fingers, reflecting the light with a brilliance that rivaled the sun itself. Her dark curls danced around her head, and the plumes of her bonnet bobbed with every step, a perfect reflection of her effervescent spirit.

Crawford couldn't help but feel his heart swell with delight as he watched his new wife's every move. Her infectious laughter echoed through the park, mingling harmoniously with the chirping of birds and the distant hum of carriages. Oh, how he longed to be the source of that laughter, to bask in the warmth of her smile. As they strolled along, Crawford's arm tucked securely around Sadie's waist, they observed the scene unfolding around them. The park was a canvas of life, bustling with couples deep in conversation, families with children racing after balls, and friends enjoying leisurely picnics on colorful blankets spread out on the lush grass.

A group of young ladies, their hats adorned with ribbons as vivid as the autumn leaves, giggled and exchanged secrets behind their gloved hands. Sadie cast a flirtatious smile at Crawford, her eyes twinkling with mischief. "Shall we join them, my lord, and see if they hold the key to all the secrets of the *ton*?"

Crawford chuckled, his deep voice laced with gentle teasing. "We are much too captivating a pair to be unleashed upon such innocent souls."

Sadie laughed delightedly, her lips forming the most enchanting of curves. "Am I to believe that my charms alone could cause such chaos?"

He pulled her closer, lowering his voice to a mere whisper. "Ah, Selkie, it is not just your charms that render me breathless. It is your wit, your spirit, and the way your eyes light up when you challenge the world with a smile."

Sadie blushed, her cheeks transforming into delicate roses.

Crawford grinned, his eyes lit with happiness and pleasure. They continued their leisurely amble, caught in a dance of words and stolen glances, surrounded by the vivid tapestry of autumn's embrace. The breeze rustled through the trees, showering them with a confetti of fallen leaves. Sadie twirled her skirts, swirling them around her in a whirl of silk and color, and Crawford followed suit, capturing her in his arms.

As they laughed and spun together, the world faded away, and in that moment, it was just the two of them, their hearts entwined amidst the splendor of nature's grandeur. Hyde Park had become their secret haven, a place where love bloomed brighter than the autumn sun, and where the promise of a future filled with joy and laughter whispered on the wind.

And so, hand in hand, they continued their journey through Hyde Park, reveling in each other's company and savoring the joyous magic that danced in the air around them.

In the ethereal twilight, they made their way home. And as Sadie's beloved Park Lane townhouse embraced the gentle caress of the growing moonlight, she and Crawford found themselves drawn to the intimacy of the house's hallowed halls. With hearts entwined, their souls ignited with a love that transcended time, they sought solace in the hidden corners of the house.

THE WARMTH OF his touch sent shivers down her spine, igniting a fire within her core. Slowly, as if time had paused to honor their union, their lips met in a kiss that spoke of a thousand whispered promises. Their mouths melded together, an exquisite harmony of longing and surrender, as their bodies swayed in a dance known only to them.

The air crackled with electricity as their hands intertwined, fingers interlacing with a delicate grace. Crawford's touch traced the curve of Sadie's waist, leaving a trail of goosebumps in its wake. With each gentle caress, their bodies pressed closer, as if they sought solace in the beating of each other's hearts.

Her breath quickened, a soft sigh escaping her lips, as Crawford's fingers delicately explored the cascading curls of her hair. So lost in the depths of her passion were they, the world around them faded into insignificance, and they were left suspended in a moment of pure bliss. They poured their souls into the tender exchange.

Time stood still in the townhouse, its walls embracing Sadie and Crawford's love and bearing witness to their stolen moment. In that alcove, their love wrote a chapter in the annals of romance, leaving an indelible mark on the fabric of their shared destiny. For within those walls, they discovered a sanctuary where love flourished, where kisses tasted of eternity, and where their hearts beat as one.

"I'm so thankful for you," Crawford whispered. "Because you make me believe. In us. In you. And in myself."

He knew he could run Castle Shipping successfully. That *they* would. With Sadie by his side, every obstacle felt small. Because his love for her was so blasted huge. And because she was a Titan of a human, a mighty warrior with the fiercest heart, all wrapped in a small package. The depth and breadth to her astounded him. Mesmerized him. Within her he saw hope and strength and courage and so very much wisdom. Something ancient and knowing only given to women of profound substance. Something well worth listening to.

And if men would bloody shut up for a moment, they could learn a lot from ladies.

Crawford had done it. He'd finally stopped, shut his mouth, and listened.

And guess what?

It was the best damn thing he ever did.

The End

About the Author

Jennifer Seasons started her career writing contemporary romances for Avon and is the author of several popular contemporary and Regency historical romances. Born in California, Jennifer has lived all over the West and now resides in the mountains of Massachusetts with her husband and their children. A dog and several cats keep them company. A lover of autumn, cozy cardigans, and coffee, Jennifer can often be found writing her novels by hand in notebooks, bundled in said cardigan with a steaming mug of dark roast nearby. When she's not writing, Jennifer enjoys running, hiking with her family, gardening, and lounging in a comfy spot with a good book and a homemade chocolate chip cookie or two.

Amazon – https://www.amazon.com/stores/Jennifer-Seasons/author/B00D8GZ5EE
Twitter – https://twitter.com/JenniferSeasons

www.ingramcontent.com/pod-product-compliance
Lightning Source LLC
Chambersburg PA
CBHW071422300726

48976CB00004B/1207